"Now you mustn't listen to the things people say about me," Jed told Kelly.

Kelly smiled nervously, then looked down at the last shrimp on her plate. She was about to attack it with her fork when Jed reached out with one hand to capture her wrist, while the other picked up the shrimp, coated it with sauce, and raised it to her mouth.

"I can feed myself," she snapped, refusing to accept the morsel from his fingers.

"Not as much fun, though." With a slow smile, he stroked the sauce-covered shrimp over her lips until her tongue instinctively darted out to lick it.

The excitement that stirred within Kelly was almost unbearable, matched only by a resurgence of her fears. Wasn't Jed too experienced for her, and bound to lose interest? Quickly she snatched the shrimp from him, almost taking his fingers with it.

"Sweetheart," he scolded with a grin, "I know your hunger for me, but try to control yourself until we're in a more private setting, okay?"

His teasing suggestion made her tremble, made her burn inside. Alone with Jed, anything could happen. . . .

WHAT ARE *LOVESWEPT* ROMANCES?

They are stories of true romance and touching emotion. We believe those two very important ingredients are constants in our highly sensual and very believable stories in the *LOVESWEPT* line. Our goal is to give you, the reader, stories of consistently high quality that may sometimes make you laugh, sometimes make you cry, but are always fresh and creative and contain many delightful surprises within their pages.

Most romance fans read an enormous number of books. Those they truly love, they keep. Others may be traded with friends and soon forgotten. We hope that each *LOVESWEPT* romance will be a treasure—a "keeper." We will always try to publish

LOVE STORIES YOU'LL NEVER FORGET
BY AUTHORS YOU'LL ALWAYS REMEMBER

The Editors

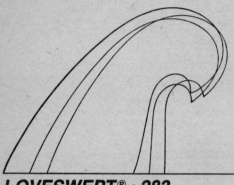

LOVESWEPT® • 283

Gail Douglas
On Wings of Flame

BANTAM BOOKS
TORONTO • NEW YORK • LONDON • SYDNEY • AUCKLAND

ON WINGS OF FLAME

A Bantam Book / October 1988

LOVESWEPT® and the wave device are registered
trademarks of Bantam Books, a division of
Bantam Doubleday Dell Publishing Group, Inc.
Registered in U.S. Patent
and Trademark Office and elsewhere.

If you would be interested in receiving protective vinyl
covers for your Loveswept books, please write to this address
for information:

Loveswept
Bantam Books
P.O. Box 985
Hicksville, NY 11802

ISBN 0-553-21937-5

Published simultaneously in the United States and Canada

Bantam Books are published by Bantam Books, a division
of Bantam Doubleday Dell Publishing Group, Inc. Its trade-
mark, consisting of the words "Bantam Books" and the
portrayal of a rooster, is Registered in U.S. Patent and
Trademark Office and in other countries. Marca Registrada.
Bantam Books, 666 Fifth Avenue, New York, New York 10103.

PRINTED IN THE UNITED STATES OF AMERICA

O   0 9 8 7 6 5 4 3 2 1

*To Dodie J.,
with thanks*

One

The familiar white mansion had loomed up in front of her too quickly, before she was ready to face the on-slaught of bittersweet memories associated with it.

Kelly Flynn sat motionless in her car for several min-utes after she had parked in the driveway beside the sprawling house. She simply wasn't ready for this.

Kelly studied the Victorian summer house that had been almost as much a part of her life once as her own family's home. Nothing about the house had changed—nothing physical, at any rate. The upstairs curtains were still frothy priscillas whose lace hems billowed through the open windows, the white clapboard siding still glistened as if its paint were only hours old, the lawn was still a lush emerald green and lovingly tended. Even the porch swing stood where it always had been, just to the left of the front door. Kelly wondered if it still creaked with the easy, soothing rhythm that haunted her dreams even now.

She forced herself to get out of the car and march toward the porch steps, absently smoothing down the skirt of her yellow linen suit. The outfit had seemed like the best choice when she'd selected it earlier, with its no-nonsense lines and crisp fabric, but now she wasn't sure. All at once she felt like a child playing grown-up in her mommy's clothes. Was the cut of the suit too severe? Too mannish? Did it overwhelm her petite figure? she wondered.

Kelly scowled. Even after seven years she was anxious for Jed Brannan's approval. Would he like her clothes? Her hair? Would he say she was beautiful?

By this time, she told herself crossly, she ought to be beyond such feminine insecurity—especially where Mr. Brannan was concerned.

She rapped sharply on the front door, startling herself with the abrupt sound. The June day was so peaceful, so quiet.

She noticed that the veranda floor was painted with gray enamel just as it should be. So far the owner hadn't succumbed to the funeral-grass craze that was littering the American landscape with garish green porches and balconies. For all his progressiveness, the heir to this house respected its traditions.

Instinctively Kelly was pleased, then annoyed with herself because she cared. She was further annoyed to catch herself patting her brown hair as if to make sure it was still on her head. And she felt a stab of irritation at the tremor that had begun in her legs and was wending its mischievous way through her body all the way to the quiver that launched an attack on her lower lip.

She bit down on her lip and knocked on the door again, hoping no one would answer. That would be a break. After all, she was doing her part, wasn't she? She'd shown up for this meeting, and right on time too. If the other party failed to appear, was that her fault? She couldn't set aside time for another appointment, so it would end here and now.

No such luck. The inner oak door opened, then the screen door.

The tall woman who smiled at Kelly had been the summer housekeeper for the Kernaghan-Brannan family for as long as Kelly could remember. Like the house, the woman hadn't changed. There wasn't one additional gray hair on the woman's head. "Kelly, dear," she said in a low voice, with the quiet authority that had always stopped Kelly in midmischief. "It's wonderful to see you here again."

Kelly stared, tongue-tied. Hadn't all those years passed? Hadn't all that pain really existed? Wasn't it the least bit awkward that Kelly Flynn was suddenly standing on the Kernaghan—now Brannan—doorstep?

Kelly had made a point, seven years ago, of avoiding this house, this street, this very neighborhood. . . . It had been no mean feat in a town as small as Traverse City, Michigan, but it had become a deeply ingrained habit. Now it was as if she'd traveled into a foreign land, a time warp, by coming here again.

Dorothy Thomas was regarding Kelly quizzically, waiting for her to say something.

"Hi," was all Kelly could manage, and even that paltry greeting sounded like the squeak of a startled chipmunk. She cleared her throat and tried for a lower pitch. "I'm here to meet . . ." Her voice failed her once more, this time because she couldn't say his name. She hadn't spoken it in seven years.

"Jed's expecting you," Dorothy said cheerfully, waving Kelly inside. "He's in his grandfather's study." The woman winced. "His study, I should say." With a heavy sigh, Dorothy shook her head sadly. "It's hard to get used to all the changes. The past months haven't been easy." She smiled at Kelly, her expression soft and compassionate. "For any of us."

To Kelly's horror, she felt her eyes fill with tears. She

hated any show of sympathy; it gave rise to feelings of self-pity, and she couldn't afford to indulge them. She blinked rapidly several times and drew a deep breath, but even the air conspired against her with its familiar scent of rich, lemon-polished wood mingled with the heady perfume of lilacs and cherry blossoms. Fragrances, like certain songs and the sound of Lake Michigan's waves washing the shore, cut right past her defenses and inevitably triggered a flood of nostalgia. She swallowed hard, trying to get rid of the sudden lump in her throat. "The study's at the rear of the house?" She didn't care that her voice sounded strained; she'd managed to say the words.

"That's right, dear. I guess you can find it on your own. I hope you don't mind, Kelly. I was just about to put bread in the oven when you knocked."

The smell of baking bread, too, Kelly thought. She smiled, realizing she was half defeated before she even met Jed. "You still bake bread?" she asked, surprised by how much calmer she sounded.

"*Some* things don't change," Dorothy replied firmly. "Not if I can help it. Oh, by the way, there is another change. Joan Walker retired when Kernaghan passed away, so Jed had to hire a new secretary. Lovely girl she is too."

Kelly's smile became a trifle forced as she squared her shoulders and headed down the hallway. *Lovely girl,* she repeated silently. Not that she cared.

She passed the broad staircase, unable to resist touching the mahogany banister, feeling its smoothness under her palm, the wood burnished by countless adult hands and naughty children's bottoms, including hers. "Don't slide down the banister!" she almost could hear echoing in the halls.

There was no one left but Dorothy to say it.

Kelly had to blink rapidly again. She shouldn't have

come. The emotions were closer to the surface than she'd realized.

She entered a small room where "Lovely Girl," a blond cherub, sat behind a desk that seemed too big for her.

The girl glanced up and her blue eyes widened. "You're Kelly Flynn. I'm Diane Grant, Jed's secretary. I've been looking forward so much to meeting you. It's funny how a person can live in such a small town and not know everybody . . ." She stood and thrust out her dainty hand. She was even tinier than Kelly, which Kelly found amazing—it didn't happen often. "I'm really thrilled to meet you, Miss Flynn. I'm sorry if I'm gushing. I promised myself I'd be cool, but you're practically famous, you know."

Kelly couldn't help smiling as she firmly gripped the girl's outstretched hand. "Actually I didn't know that," she said, bemused by the greeting.

Diane laughed. "Well, maybe not *People* magazine famous, but you're a celebrity around northern Michigan. In certain circles, anyway. I don't know what I did for gifts before you came out with your Shamrock Specialties line. I've bought more baby quilts . . . and those terrific aprons that are so whimsical. I gave my boyfriend, or rather my ex-boyfriend, one of the tuxedo-style ones, the kind with the bow tie that lights up? He loved it. And everybody in my family has at least a couple of Christmas decorations you designed. I have to admit I can't afford your full-size quilts yet, but they did inspire me to start doing some quilting myself. Not original designs like yours, of course. Plain log-cabin fare for me, I'm afraid, and believe me, that's a challenge! Where on earth do you find so many brilliant ideas? And how do you manage to produce so *much*?"

Kelly was fascinated by the girl's ability to talk nonstop, without taking a single breath. It was positively amazing. Several seconds passed before the questions registered. "Oh," she said, not sure how to respond. It was her first interview, and she really didn't know the answers. The second question was easier to handle so she tackled it first. "I *don't* produce it all. I just create the designs, you know. Seamstresses do the actual work."

"Even so," the secretary insisted. "Coming up with the designs is the hard part, it really is. And now you're even working with stained glass. I saw some of your work in a gallery in Petoskey last weekend. It's just fantastic! What I'd give for a talent like yours."

Kelly was enjoying the admiration, but she wasn't sure how to react to it. "Once again," she admitted, feeling guilty that she was getting all the credit when her contribution was only one step in the whole process, "I only do the designs and make the patterns. Artisans actually work with the stained glass itself."

Diane laughed again. "You're much too modest. But you still haven't given me a clue about where you get your ideas. They're so different!"

Kelly hesitated. She'd hoped Diane had forgotten that question, because she didn't have a concrete answer. Where did she get her ideas? From everywhere. Finally she thought of a major source of her inspiration. "For one thing," she said seriously, "I comb books on heraldry and mythology and religions of the world to find symbols I can stylize and incorporate into a design."

"Like the Celtic cross," Diane stated.

Kelly had to grin. "You really are up-to-date with what I'm doing." That stained-glass piece had been completed only a couple of weeks ago. She was beginning to like having a fan, and she searched for more hints she could pass on to the girl.

Then the secretary shattered Kelly's rosy glow by returning to reality. "I should tell Jed you're here. He's the one you came to meet, not me."

Kelly wanted to say she was quite content with the present company. There was no need to tell the boss anything. After a little visit with Diane she'd be happy to be on her way.

But she smiled and nodded, too proud to retreat. "I've enjoyed talking with you," she said shyly.

"Well, I'm sure we'll have lots of opportunities to chat again," Diane said, then knocked on the thick oak door of the study. Without waiting for a response, she pushed the door open. "Kelly Flynn's here, Jed," she announced with surprising informality.

Kelly felt a shimmer of apprehension, not only because the moment she'd dreaded was upon her, but because of Diane Grant's offhand remark. Why would there be lots of opportunities for chats? What was Jed Brannan up to? What had he told his secretary?

More to the point, Kelly admitted to herself, why had she agreed to the meeting? How could she have believed that the years had matured her enough to face this man without falling apart, as if he were merely another client?

Murmuring her thanks to Diane, Kelly entered the high-ceilinged, oak-paneled inner sanctum of Jed's office. As the door closed behind her she froze, feeling as if she'd landed in the middle of a Gothic melodrama. Unfortunately, she realized, she didn't have the qualities of a spunky heroine. She thought she was going to be sick.

Jed stood behind his desk, surveying her with his dark eyes. "Kelly," he said softly, sounding almost surprised she had come.

His voice was like the fragrances, the songs, the waves on the shore: It cut right past her defenses to the long-buried ache inside her.

She stared at him, unable to move, barely able to breathe. How could a face be so familiar, she asked herself, yet so oddly foreign? His gray eyes were as mesmerizing as she remembered, his lips as inviting, his sandy hair as silky. Yet the overall impact was dramatically altered. Jed's features, always sculpted by an uncompromising hand, were no longer even slightly boyish. Their clean lines had been roughened by the years and probably more than a few brawls, his skin tanned and weathered by desert sun and Arctic winds. A bump on the bridge of his nose marred its original perfection, but beneath it his smile was still mischievous, warm, gentle.

Kelly's gaze slid downward to Jed's chest, once lean but now filled out to unexpected breadth. His shoulders had never been narrow, but they'd developed a new, awesome muscularity, and his arms clearly acquired a steely strength that the blue polo shirt he wore emphasized.

Impossible. Jed Brannan was more gorgeous than ever. It wasn't fair. He should have been balding and paunchy, or at least have gone to seed a little. There was absolutely no justice. Kelly was ready to forsake pride and dignity to bolt from the room and run for her life.

As she gaped at Jed, his gaze traveled over her, taking in her petite form with feminine curves that were inadequately disguised by her tailored suit and print blouse. Her wavy brown hair was shorter than it was a week ago when he'd caught a fleeting glimpse of her in town. He wondered if she'd had it cut in time for this encounter knowing how he'd always loved her hair long. If she had, the ploy hadn't worked. He liked the way the shiny strands caressed her delicate jawline. Her new look suited her.

Her skin was so creamy, He hadn't exaggerated its flawlessness during those long nights when he'd dreamed of touching her. At the moment, her cheeks were flagged with bright pink, a sure sign of high emotion. Kelly's feelings always showed, he remembered, though it was sometimes difficult to know whether she was enflamed by passion, fury, or excitement—or all three. He'd give anything for the answer to that particular riddle. His fingers tightened around the pencil he was holding until it snapped.

Kelly kept staring at him, her full, soft lips slightly parted, her eyes swimming with emotions Jed couldn't fathom however hard he tried. "So it's true," he murmured, thinking aloud. "Those eyes are the very color of your name. I've seen fields of Ireland less green."

Kelly blinked. Her heart began pounding, and she prayed Jed wouldn't hear it. She couldn't let him know how he affected her. She just couldn't. In fact she flatly refused to let him beguile her with his glib Irish charm. "You wanted to see me for a reason other than an eye examination?" she asked.

Jed chuckled, taken aback by her cheekiness but delighted by it. She was still the Kelly he'd fallen in love with. "Straight to the point, is it?"

"I have no time to conduct business any other way," she told him in a deliberately formal manner.

This isn't going to be easy, he thought, wondering if he was going to make a fool of himself. Kelly was worth the gamble, he decided. He moved toward her, covering the distance between them with three strides of his long legs, barely noticing the barrier of the desk as he skirted it. "You'll at least sit down while we talk, won't you?"

Kelly was tempted to refuse but decided it would seem childish, so she let him show her to a comfortable leather armchair, pressing her elbows close to her side when he seemed about to touch her.

Jed saw the instinctive gesture and pulled back his hand, sighing inwardly. This wasn't going to be easy at all. "Coffee?" he offered, going to a table in front of one book-lined wall. He took the carafe from the coffee maker and held it up as if ready to pour at the instant she gave the command.

"No, thank you," Kelly said. She sat with her ankles crossed, knees together, back ramrod straight. She folded her hands in her lap and waited for Jed to explain why he'd asked her to come.

He put the carafe back, his spirits plummeting faster than a water balloon from a twentieth-floor window. "I won't have any either," he muttered. "I drink too much of the stuff." He forced himself to grin at Kelly, making a stab at lightheartedness. "Not such a terrible vice, though, drinking coffee—for an Irishman, anyway."

Kelly surprised him by rising to the bait. "I'm sure you have more colorful vices, Brannan." She was positive he could hear the thump of her heart, and had she developed a nervous tic? Just under her right eye, it was. She tried to turn so he wouldn't see it.

He drew his thick eyebrows together in a straight line. His forehead was creased by a sudden frown. "What's this 'Brannan' business?"

Kelly forgot to hide her tic. She stared in shock, realizing what she'd done. The name had slipped out, the result of another silly habit she'd developed during those first weeks . . . those years . . . after he'd left. She'd refused even to think of the name she'd whispered so lovingly in his ear. "Jed" was too intimate, too sweet, too redolent of happy moments that were gone forever. So she'd begun thinking of him as "Brannan," somehow feeling distanced from him with the verbal trick. But she wasn't about to tell him that. "I . . . I guess it's because you've inherited the mantle of your grandfather. Everyone called him by his last name, so it seems natural to do the same with you." She was proud of her quick thinking. Perhaps maturity was of some use after all.

Jed perched on the corner of his desk and studied her. "You used to call me Jed," he said quietly. "I liked the sound of my first name on your lips."

How dare he, Kelly fumed silently. He was the one who'd walked out, and he hadn't paused then to hear the sound of his name on her lips.

She held her temper in check. She was older now. He couldn't affect her as he once had. With a great effort she spoke in a perfectly calm voice. "What is the reason for this meeting?"

"No small talk allowed? No catching up on the past seven years? No renewal of an old acquaintance?" Jed teased, prodding her deliberately, hoping to force some honest show of emotion from her even if it was anger.

"I hardly think that would be necessary, Brannan," Kelly replied, determined not to let him get to her.

He laughed. "So you're still stubborn, are you?" Suddenly he sobered and a pained expression crossed his features as he looked at her. "But I suppose you've needed to be stubborn. You've been through some rough times." He moved from the desk to an armchair opposite Kelly's and settled into it, deciding to change the tone of the conversation if he could. "How's your brother?"

Kelly was thrown slightly by the question, but she answered politely. "Michael's doing quite well, thank you."

"Nineteen now, isn't he? Studying music?"

Kelly's pride in her younger brother overshadowed her wariness of Jed, though she was surprised by his knowledge. "Mike's a violinist," she told him, glad she didn't have to say "Mike's a dropout," or "Mike's acquired a nasty drug dependency," or "Mike's gone . . . I don't know where." He had been so close, so terrifyingly close. Now she could honestly brag. "He'll be at Interlochen all summer."

"And Juilliard in the fall?" Jed added.

Kelly's wariness returned. "Why all the interest in my brother's education?"

"Simply because he's your brother. And, for the past couple of years, your responsibility. It's a heavy load for such fragile shoulders."

"Not so fragile, Brannan. And there's enough insurance money to pay for Mike's education."

"You sold the house too."

"I had no need for it."

"But you loved it, Kelly. You were happy there. It must have torn you apart to give it up."

"It was something that had to be done. I'm not the only person in the world who ever had to make a difficult decision."

Jed leaned forward, resting his elbows on his knees and loosely clasping his hands. "Kelly, I didn't hear about your parents until months after the accident. I can't tell you how sorry I am."

Before she could quell it, the instinct to seek Jed's comfort washed over her. She wanted to lean against the hard wall of his chest, feel his strong arms holding her, bury her face in the warmth of his throat.

But she wasn't a little girl anymore, and she didn't need anyone's comfort, she realized. She'd gotten through the past two years since her mother and father were killed by a drunk driver on the highway, and she'd gotten through those years without leaning on a man. "You have your own grief to deal with right now," she reminded Jed in a low voice, offering understanding of his pain while shutting him out of sharing in her own.

Jed knew what she was doing, but realized it was too soon to try to penetrate the shield she'd erected around herself. "Dorothy said you were at Kernaghan's funeral. I guess I was too broken up to see anyone." *Broken up* was a mild term; he'd nearly collapsed at the news of his grandfather's sudden heart attack. For some reason he'd expected the old man to live forever. Eighty years old was a ripe age to live to, but it wasn't even close to forever. And the fact that Kernaghan had gone quickly and quietly was small comfort. He shouldn't have gone at all. Jed still couldn't accept it.

Kelly averted her gaze; the grief in Jed's eyes was too raw. Once, the two of them had expected to face all life's tragedies together. It hadn't worked out that way, however. Neither of them could have imagined at the time how many terrible moments they'd have to face, or how soon. "So Dorothy's staying on with you," she said, switching to a more mundane topic.

Jed smiled. "She says I need her. I think she's right."

"You don't need anyone," Kelly blurted out. She couldn't keep all her bitterness buried. There was just too much inside her.

Jed sat back in his chair and studied her. "Is that what you really think?"

Not choosing to respond, Kelly fixed her attention on the bookshelves lining the room's east wall, then found the computer in the opposite corner of extreme interest.

"You're wrong, Kelly," he said, his voice strained. "You don't know how wrong."

She was on dangerous ground, she realized. Jed could easily appeal to her sense of compassion, especially when she knew how close he'd been to his grandfather. Then there were all those lonely nights he probably would claim to have suffered through during his travels. Not many nights, she was willing to wager. She vowed *not* to soften toward him, not to show it, anyway. "Perhaps that's true," she agreed superficially. "Perhaps I'm wrong. Even you have needed help occasionally. Even you couldn't battle those kidnappers in Lebanon all by yourself." Kelly fought a sudden surge of heartsickness at the thought of how close Jed had come to disaster. He owed his life to a pair of heroic marines who'd happened along at the crucial moment. "But it would take something drastic like that," she managed to go on, "to make you the least bit vulnerable to anything or anybody."

"It took a situation like that," Jed replied slowly, every word vibrating with emotion, "to start me thinking, making a few overdue decisions about what matters most to me." Suddenly he scowled at her as a thought struck him. "How did you know about that incident? It wasn't publicized."

Kelly cursed herself and tried to brush off the evidence of her interest in his adventures. "Oh, Kernaghan used to go on and on about his grandson the real-life Indiana Jones."

"And you made time to listen," Jed pointed out softly.

She was getting herself in deeper by the minute, Kelly thought with annoyance. "Your grandfather was a good friend to me and to my brother," she explained truthfully, then added not quite so honestly, "so the least I could do was put up with his boasting about you."

Jed turned away so Kelly couldn't see his tiny, pleased smile. Kernaghan was right: She hadn't stopped caring. "In that case," he continued as soon as he could look at Kelly again without his elation showing, "perhaps I can count on you to do something else for my grandfather, and accept the assignment I want to offer you."

"What assignment? What could I do that would . . . ?"

"Patience, Kelly," Jed said, then took a deep breath before he forged ahead with what suddenly seemed absolutely ridiculous to him. "First you have to promise not to laugh."

"I'm not in a laughing mood, Brannan."

"For crying out loud," he said in a sharp voice. "*Will* you use my name? You've made your point with this 'Brannan' nonsense. It's getting on my nerves."

Kelly smiled sweetly. "*Will* you get to the point, Brannan? This whole interview is getting on *my* nerves."

Jed's eyes narrowed. He'd forgotten how stubborn she could be. Maybe it would be smarter to do as she asked and get to the point—the real point. Maybe he should forget the ruse of this so-called assignment, he thought, and just haul her into his arms and find out once and for all how she really felt.

Kelly shifted uneasily in her chair, wondering if she'd pushed Jed too far. She didn't know him at all; this man wasn't the Jed she'd loved so desperately . . . so hopelessly. "Well?" she prompted in a voice that was smaller and more tentative than she liked.

Jed saw her nervousness and realized he'd become a stranger to her, a stranger who made her a little afraid. He took another deep breath and tried it Kernaghan's way. "I'd like you to do a stained-glass portrait."

"Of whom?" she asked, surprised by the innocuousness of his words.

"Of Beau," Jed answered, pausing to wait for understanding to follow disbelief in Kelly's expressive features. "You do remember Beauregarde?" he added as two little furrows appeared between Kelly's eyebrows. He'd always loved those furrows.

Kelly stared at him, then burst out laughing.

Jed pretended to be hurt. "You promised you wouldn't laugh."

Kelly couldn't help it. Her nerves had been stretched to the breaking point since Jed's secretary had called. She composed herself. "All right, I laughed. Sorry. But really, J—" She cleared her throat. "Really, Brannan. A portrait of that dumb bird?"

Jed heard the near slip and his spirits lifted. His game might work, weird as it seemed. "Look, Kelly, my grandfather was crazy about that bird, who, by the way, is definitely not dumb. Rude, yes. Loud mouthed . . ."

"Loud beaked," Kelly corrected.

Jed suppressed a grin. "Loud beaked, then." How he'd missed his saucy little Kelly Flynn. How he'd dreamed of coming home to find her. How he'd hurt when he thought he'd lost her forever. Only characters in fairy tales and Greek tragedies loved one person for as long as seven years. He had no right to harbor the slightest hope of regaining a love that had been stupidly thrown away. His grin broadened as he warmed to his subject. "Beauregarde is more demanding than ten kids, Kelly, but he was Kernaghan's buddy. He's more raucous than a heavy-metal rock group, and he's a chauvinist besides. I can't—"

"A chauvinist?"Kelly interrupted, getting caught up in the ridiculous conversation. "Male chauvinist?"

"You'll see. He's disgusting."

"Now where could that bird have picked up such attitudes?" Kelly said in her most saccharine tone. "Not in the midst of *this* family of enlightened males, certainly."

Jed nodded. "I have to admit that Kernaghan had some pretty old-fashioned ideas about women."

"Which he passed on to the bird?"

"I'm afraid so."

"And now you're asking me to enshrine this male chauvinist parrot in stained glass like some kind of saint?"

Jed drew himself up, pretending to be insulted. "Beau is not a parrot. He's a mynah bird."

Kelly shrugged. "Whatever." Getting to her feet, she

offered Jed a cool smile, realizing that she'd come perilously close to laughing with him; it took her back to happier times that couldn't be recaptured. "I'm afraid I'll have to decline your fascinating assignment, Brannan. I don't do bird portraits." She gathered up her purse and made herself look at Jed, wondering if it would be the last time. Surely he wouldn't stay in Traverse City Surely it was much too small for him now. With her smile pasted in place, she spoke with all the disdain she could muster. "I especially don't do bird portraits when I'm opposed to the subject's social philosophies. Good-bye, Brannan. It's been great."

Jed watched, stunned, as Kelly prepared to march out of the room and out of his life, again.

Two

Jed's paralysis didn't last long. Suddenly he bolted from his chair. "No!" he blurted. "You can't!"

Kelly paused, taken aback by the intensity of his statement. He was leaning over his desk, palms flat, body thrust forward as if he were ready to vault over if she tried to leave. "Can't what?" she demanded.

Can't go, he thought desperately. *Not yet. Not before I've even had a chance.* "Can't refuse," he said aloud.

Kelly shook her head. "Same old Jed Brannan. He gives an order and expects it to be obeyed. Well, not this time, Brannan. I don't jump to your tune any more."

"Dance," he muttered, automatically correcting her.

"What are you talking about?" Kelly asked, momentarily deterred from leaving.

"Dance to my tune. Jump to my command. You always did scramble your clichés."

Blue flames flared in the emerald depths of Kelly's eyes. "Dancing, jumping—who cares? The point is, I *can* refuse to do that stupid bird picture, and I *am* refusing!" She whirled around to leave the room.

In a panic Jed rushed after her. Gently but firmly he turned her by the shoulders and placed her very neatly in her chair again.

She glared at him, shocked and livid. "You're out of line, mister." Her voice was low and threatening, though she wished she could get rid of the tremor his touch had set off. "I won't stand for it," she added in a menacing tone, as much to her weaker self as to Jed.

He himself was taken aback by his impulsive Tarzan approach, but it was too late. He had to bluff through it. "Good. What I want you to do is sit for it."

"Corny, Brannan." Kelly wrinkled her pert nose. "You were always corny." Her temper was fueled by the warmth that was coursing through her veins, melting her resistance to Jed Brannan. "You're as much a male chauvinist as that parrot," she told him, sounding braver than she felt. "But this is one lady who doesn't quail in fear."

Jed laughed heartily. "Quail? You make an awful pun like that and you dare to call me corny?"

"Stop making fun of me, dammit!" She tried to spring from her chair, but Jed grinned and gently pushed her down again.

Kelly's outrage was complete. "Drop the strong-arm stuff, Brannan," she said through clenched teeth, "or I'll deliver a swift kick where it'll do the most good." As she spoke she arched her back and thrust out her chin defiantly. "Read my lips, all right? I am going to leave now. I am refusing your plum assignment, despite an artistic challenge unequaled since Michelangelo learned how to paint upside down. I am not interested, and you do not scare me. Do I make myself clear?"

Jed thought about kissing her, if only to shut her up, but he knew how Kelly acted when she was mad. She might just bite off his lip. "Will you please listen to me for one minute?" he asked.

Kelly crossed her arms over her chest like a bratty six-year-old. "No."

Jed's own temper was stirring. He'd tried to hold it down, but Kelly could be so impossible. "You have to listen," he told her, "unless you plan to add to your childish repertoire by putting your hands over your ears."

"You overbearing . . ." No adequate insult came to mind. "You and your kind think you can—"

"My kind?" Jed interrupted. "What does that mean?"

"Men!" Kelly shouted. "And if you'll pardon my bigotry, Irishmen in particular!"

"I've always pardoned your bigotry!" Jed yelled back, losing control at last. "And your stubbornness. And your tantrums, and your—"

"Oh, would you listen to his silver tongue," Kelly crooned. "Why, he's a veritable bard, he is. No wonder I was enthralled in my youth and innocence. No wonder I'd have done anything he asked of me—"

"Except grow up," Jed said. She'd gotten to him, just as she'd been able to do in the past. With everyone else he could believe he was easygoing, even placid, that his notorious Irish hot-bloodedness was a myth—but not with this woman around. "I thought . . . I hoped . . you might have matured enough to understand why I left seven years ago. But no. You're still nursing your wounded female pride."

"Ha! Don't flatter yourself, Brannan. I couldn't care less about what happened a lifetime ago. I'm glad you left. I surely wouldn't want to be saddled now with an arrogant, egotistical, domineering"—she hesitated, then settled for the summary of all his faults—"Irishman!"

Jed leaned down, placing his hands on the back of Kelly's chair to surround her small body with his arms. "But that's the point," he said, suddenly calm again.

"What? What's the point? That you're arrogant, egotistical, and domineering? Or that you're an Irishman? The words, after all, are symony . . . synomyn . . ." She cursed under her breath; her temper always undermined her eloquence.

Jed couldn't suppress a chuckle. "Synonymous," he supplied. "If you insist on flinging insults at my ancestry—and your own, I feel obliged to point out—try using easier words. Stick to two syllables or less."

Kelly would have bargained seriously with Lucifer to have seen Jed trip over the word syllable, but he didn't, so she decided to take his advice. She opened her mouth to launch into a litany of insults that were two syllables or less.

This time Jed did kiss her, lightly and quickly. He wasn't taking any chances. "The point is, girl," he said once he'd stunned her into silence, "you were eighteen. You deserved a better life than one spent trailing after me. You'd have hated the places I've been, and you'd have missed the chance to fulfill your own talent. By now you'd have been resentful and frustrated."

"You didn't have to go," Kelly said in a small voice.

"I did have to go, Kelly, and you know it." Jed crouched down until his eyes were level with hers. He spoke gently, persuasively, taking one of her delicate hands between his two palms. He was grateful when she didn't pull away from him. "Kernaghan's company started small," he explained, though they'd been through the same discussions years ago without ever coming to an understanding. "My grandfather grew with his company. It wasn't very diversified or huge when my father got involved, but by the time he decided to play middle-aged hippie, Kernaghan Explorations had investments and projects all over the world. Kernaghan was a vital man, but I knew even he couldn't carry on forever. I was nominated because there was no one else."

"And because you wanted it," Kelly added.

Jed nodded. "Yes. I wanted it. I won't pretend otherwise. I was fully aware what I'd have to do to fill Kernaghan's shoes—or at least to try. I had to learn the ropes from the ground up. I had to understand the workings of those North Sea oil rigs and the complexities of negotiating styles among people from South America to the Middle East. Could I have learned it from a safe nest in Traverse City, Kelly? Could I have given you all the love you deserved while I was flying all over the world?"

Kelly averted her face so Jed couldn't see the tears welling up in her eyes. They were rehashing ancient history. None of it mattered now.

Then she heard her voice saying words that horrified her. "I could have gone with you. I was strong enough to have handled it."

Jed closed his eyes and took a deep breath. She still cared. "You probably were strong enough," he conceded softly. "But I didn't know it then."

Startled by his admission, Kelly stared at him and immediately regretted it. His lips were just inches from hers, tantalizing her. His warm breath fanned her skin while his gaze caressed her with a familiar possessiveness that thrilled her.

She sank down into her chair. She didn't want to be thrilled by him. His effect on her hadn't lost a bit of its potency, and she knew she was as vulnerable to him now as she'd been since the first time she'd laid eyes on him when she was fifteen.

Jed saw the way she recoiled. Stung, he released her hand and straightened up. So he'd been kidding himself, he thought miserably. Kelly didn't want anything to do with him. She was finished with him. He was making a fool of himself.

He moved back behind his desk and sank into the oversize leather chair. Swiveling from side to side, he fidgeted with the two ends of the pencil he'd broken earlier, absently trying to fit the pieces together again. It didn't work. "I'm sorry," he said with a rasp in his voice. "I didn't ask you to come here so we could start quarreling where we left off seven years ago." Suddenly he felt like a complete usurper, sitting in Kernaghan's chair at Kernaghan's desk, trying to be everything his grandfather had been: powerful, tender, daring, fun loving, clever. He wasn't sure he had it in him. Kernaghan could have won Kelly back with a word. For that matter, he probably wouldn't have lost her in the first place. He'd have found a way to keep her love in the face of all obstacles. "Sorry," he repeated.

Kelly stood slowly, carefully, trembling in every part of her being. "So I'm allowed to leave now?" she asked, trying to sound playful but managing only to seem brusque.

Jed threw down the pencil pieces and picked up a gold pen with Kernaghan's name engraved on it. No doubt it was the pen the old man had used to write the letter that had turned out to be his last—the letter that had inspired this misguided meeting with Kelly. Rolling the pen between his fingers, Jed studied it intently as he spoke. "Thanks for coming over to give me a fair hearing, anyhow."

Kelly nodded, but couldn't think of another thing to say. So that was it. She wouldn't do the portrait of Beauregarde, and the interview was over, just like that. There was nothing else Jed wanted of her. Nothing more to say. Thanks for coming over, nice to see you, good-bye.

She turned and walked toward the study door, trying to tell herself she was relieved. She'd faced the dragon in his den and she'd survived. Granted, her body felt as if an electric charge had sizzled through her, leaving her very pores crackling with an acute aliveness she'd forgotten she could feel. Granted, she suspected that if she went back to the privacy and solitude of her little beach cottage, she'd start crying and stop in perhaps a decade or two. Granted, her legs were heavy and aching and protesting vehemently against every step she took in a direction away from Jed Brannan. Nevertheless, she was relieved. "Good-bye," she whispered as she put her hand on the doorknob.

Jed's inner being contracted into a tight ball and then he exploded in protest. He refused to lose her again! Not without a battle that would make the Clash of the Titans look like a wine-and-cheese party. With not a shred of shame he played his trump card. "Bye, Kelly. I'm sorry it worked out this way. I wish you'd agreed to do Beau's portrait, but I respect your decision. I couldn't help hoping, since it *was* Kernaghan's last request, but . . ."

Kelly turned to face him. "His last request? Is that true?"

Well, almost, Jed thought, troubled by a tiny pang of guilt. It was true that Kernaghan had suggested commissioning Kelly to do a stained-glass panel starring Beauregarde, and it was true that the letter in which he'd made the suggestion was the last he'd ever written. Kelly didn't have to know that the idea was one of Kernaghan's matchmaking schemes, "an excuse to see the stubborn girl and soften her up," as he'd put it.

So Jed nodded at Kelly. "Don't be influenced by that," he told her with feigned sincerity. "It was eccentric of my grandfather. You can't take responsibility for his crazy request."

Kelly moved toward the desk, her expression guarded. "I don't recall noticing any other signs of Kernaghan's eccentricity."

Jed thought fast. "Well, how *would* you notice? He was always a little . . . different. I mean, how many men do you know who dyed their white hair and mustache green on St. Patrick's Day and orange on Orangemen's Day?"

Kelly's lips quirked up in an unbidden smile. "He wasn't being eccentric, he was making a political statement. He deplored the hatreds of the old country."

Jed felt as if a huge burden had been lifted from his heart. He realized it was Kernaghan's charm that was getting through to Kelly, not his own. He didn't care. "And what kind of political statement was he making when he dyed his hair scarlet for Valentine's Day?"

This time Kelly actually laughed. "He did that out of pure romanticism. Besides, he just liked to shake people up sometimes, especially the small-town locals of Traverse City."

Another sensitive subject, Jed warned himself: the locals versus what Kelly called the summer people. The wealthy vacationers from places like Detroit, New York, and Chicago, who flooded the area every spring with yachts and fat billfolds and superior attitudes. Kelly was a local; the Kernaghans and Brannans were "summer people." He had one strike against him. He chose to ignore her remark. "Anyway, Kelly, whether he was eccentric or not, I don't want you to feel obligated to enshrine Beau in stained glass, as you put it, unless you feel comfortable about it. You were right earlier. I was out of line."

"Why didn't you tell me it was his last request?"

Why indeed, Jed thought, then was inspired. "I didn't want to lay that kind of guilt on you."

She accepted his explanation, then had second thoughts. "So why tell me now?"

All at once Jed could visualize his mother wagging her finger at him. "When first we practice to deceive . . ." she would say. He cleared his throat. "It struck me that I didn't have the right to let you walk out of here without telling you how much Kernaghan admired your work." *Credible*, he congratulated himself, *quite credible.*

Kelly chewed on her lower lip, thinking. Really, the job didn't have to involve seeing a lot of Jed. She could work from a quick sketch of the bird—better still, a snapshot. It wasn't as if she had to capture minute facial expressions. "I can hardly refuse after all, can I?"

At that moment Jed experienced an unbelievable rush of affection for the miserable bird, but he played the game cautiously. "I don't want you to feel obligated, Kelly."

She scowled at him, trying to figure out his plan. "Do you want me to do it or not?"

"I want you to," he answered hastily.

"I hope you realize that my work is stylized, not realistic. I might not do what you want, or what Kernaghan envisioned."

Jed smiled. If he had his way, she'd do exactly what he wanted and what Kernaghan envisioned. "I do realize your work is stylized. I think it's wonderful."

"You do?" she questioned. "What do you know? "

Offended, he got to his feet and looked down his nose at her. "I'm not completely uncultivated, Kelly. I've been to the Louvre. I know a Picasso from a Rembrandt, a cubist from an impressionist, even."

"I mean," Kelly said, rolling her eyes, "what do you know of my work?"

At last he was on safe ground. He could answer honestly, because he did know Kelly's work. The Louvre wasn't the only gallery he'd visited. Besides a few in London, New York, and Madrid, he'd spent infinitely more fascinating hours combing the shops and galleries of northern Michigan since his return to the area three months ago. The unusual gift items of Kelly's Shamrock Specialties line amused and delighted him, but he'd more than once found himself stunned by the bold imagination displayed in one of Kelly's quilt designs and, more recently, her stained-glass panels.

During all the years he'd been away he'd never really gotten over her, though he'd wandered through a few relationships in a lame attempt to forget her. Then, even after he returned home, even after all Kernaghan's praise of Kelly, Jed hadn't let himself believe the magic of their youthful love could be re-created.

Though their paths had never actually crossed, he'd caught an occasional glimpse of her on the street or at the tennis club where they both were members.

He'd realized immediately that Kelly hadn't changed much, except for the fact she possessed more of every quality he'd loved in her. She was more appealingly fresh with her dewy complexion and pink-tinged cheeks, more desirable with her petite, feminine curves, more intriguing with her boundless energy and unfailing cheerfulness.

It was the discovery of her use of ancient Celtic symbolism that had knocked him for a loop. For five years he'd been drawn to the pagan and early Christian lore of his forebears; the study of it had gone beyond a hobby with him and had become almost a second vocation. To find that Kelly had gravitated toward the same subject made him feel as if the two of them had remained connected all along in some mysterious way. An inner sensation of belonging to her, of knowing she belonged to him, had always been a strong element in his love for Kelly. He felt as though they'd been part of each other for all time, two halves that searched endlessly until they could reunite to form a single entity.

Kelly watched Jed, wondering what he was thinking as he gazed silently at her. "What do you know of my work?" she asked again.

"The Celtic cross," he murmured. "The White Horse. The god Cernunnos."

The Celtic cross was easy, Kelly thought, not quite believing what she'd just heard. Jed's secretary had mentioned it too. Even the White Horse was named in the quilt's description. But for Jed to identify the strange figure she'd used as the basis of her last stained-glass panel . . . "I didn't name the subject in the title," she said aloud. "Or in the gallery's catalogue."

Jed didn't answer her. There would be time enough for explanations. He thought of the years they'd lost, when they could have been sharing this passion along with others. "So you'll do the portrait?" he finally asked.

Kelly nodded.

"I have your word?" He didn't want to leave anything vague between them.

"You have my word."

"One more thing, Kelly." Jed moved to stand close to her and crooked his index finger under her chin. "Go back to calling me Jed, will you?"

Kelly stood motionless, caught in the spell he'd always been able to cast over her. Her lips parted slightly and her body swayed toward him. She caught herself before it was too late. "Don't push your luck, Brannan," she said, stepping away from him.

Jed sighed heavily and dropped his hand to his side. Kelly Flynn was going to be quite a challenge. "We haven't discussed your fee," he reminded her.

"I don't charge a fee for honoring last requests," Kelly said, heading for the door, but this time with a lighter heart.

"I'll pay you a fee whether you charge one or not," Jed insisted, following her.

"I won't accept it."

"You will."

Kelly shot him a pleading look. "Can we postpone this argument? I have other appointments."

Jed grinned and opened the door for her. "When can you get started?"

"I'll check my work schedule and let you know," Kelly said, brushing past him. She was playing for time. She knew her schedule all too well, but she wanted to find a way to do the job without seeing Jed again. Her vulnerability to his charm had been too apparent to her for her to risk encountering him any more than necessary.

Jed turned to his secretary, who looked up from her typewriter. "Diane, I'll just walk Kelly to her car."

"That isn't necessary," Kelly protested.

Jed ignored her. "Kelly will be calling to set up a time for a . . ." He smiled at Kelly. "What would you call it? A sitting? A perching, maybe?"

She gave him a forced smile. "A photo opportunity. I'll just snap his little picture a few times and go from there."

Jed experienced a prickle of disappointment. He'd hoped Kelly would spend several lengthy sessions trying to capture in sketches the essence of Beauregarde's dubious charisma. "Well, whatever," he said, turning back to speak to Diane. "Anyway, Kelly will be giving you a call. You two can make arrangements?"

"Sure," Diane replied cheerfully. "I think we can stumble our way to an appointment without your supervision."

Kelly's eyes widened in surprise. She expected Jed to be annoyed at the girl's disrespect, but he just muttered to himself: "Cheeky females. Why do I surround myself with them?"

He put his hand on the small of Kelly's back to guide her through the house toward the front door. Her pulse skipped a beat and then raced. Acutely aware that Jed Brannan was a dangerous man, she resolved to be immune to him. He'd hurt her once; she wasn't going to give him a second shot at it.

As they stepped out onto the front porch, Kelly's gaze was drawn to the swing. She tried to look away before Jed could see her reaction to the feelings of nostalgia that tore through her, but she was too late.

He slid his hand around her waist and pulled her closer to his side. "We've spent a few hours there, haven't we?" he murmured.

Kelly nodded, but couldn't speak, overwhelmed by memories of happier, more uncomplicated times.

Jed felt the depth of her anguish as if it were his own. So many things had changed since the days when they whiled away their evenings surrounded by the scent of cherry blossoms and the tang of a Great Lakes breeze. Kelly had lost a great deal. So had he, but she was much more alone than he was. He still had a mother, a father of sorts somewhere, and now a likable stepfather too. "You work from home, I understand," he remarked in an effort to distract Kelly from her thoughts.

She looked up at him in surprise. He knew a lot about her. "I prefer it. I like to work late at night with no interruptions." *Fewer, anyway,* she thought, recalling the recent scourge of midnight phone calls. "And it keeps the overhead down. That's important in the kind of cottage industry I've set up."

"And knowing you," Jed added, "you'd rather pay your free-lance workers well than set yourself up in fancy corporate headquarters. Your place is a cottage on the beach, isn't it? On the northern approach to town?"

"Yes, it is." *Too much,* Kelly thought. He knew too much. *Why?* she wondered. He didn't move in circles where she'd be the subject of idle gossip. The summer people didn't concern themselves much with the locals.

More memories were stirred up from the ashes of the past as Kelly's gaze was caught by Jed's. She saw in his eyes the two of them walking along the shore of Lake Michigan, laughing as their bare feet splashed in the cool water, hands clasped with the easy confidence of a young couple in love. Somehow they had always found their way to a secluded cove seen only by winking stars and moonlight that shimmered like molten gold over the lake's surface. Inevitably they caressed and kissed until their passions carried them to wild, dizzying heights, and they sank to the waiting sand, aching for the union that promised to be their only release.

But Jed always stopped, always kept his head even when Kelly was past the point of no return. It was always Jed who took a deep breath, stood and drew Kelly to her feet to lead her back to a public place. It was always Kelly who lost control; always Jed who kept it.

She closed her eyes to shut out the images, and for the second time she heard herself speak without thinking. "Why didn't you make love to me?" she asked, immediately mortified by her own question. Her eyes flew open in disbelief. She hadn't said that. She couldn't have said that!

"You were eighteen," Jed answered, amazed she needed the explanation. "I was twenty-five. How much of a rat do you think I was, anyway?"

Kelly wanted to escape. She felt like a complete idiot. "You wouldn't like to know," she muttered, and headed down the steps.

Jed's hand shot out and circled around her upper arm, stopping her in midstep. "You think I didn't want you, right? You've built it up in your head that I stayed in control without any trouble at all. You think you were the only one who was frustrated."

"Did I say any of that?" Kelly asked.

"Damn right you did. Just now. Your big green eyes are even more eloquent than your saucy tongue, girl."

Kelly wished she could stop liking the way Jed lapsed into an Irish lilt when his emotions were aroused. She'd tried for years to tell herself the brogue was an affectation, since Jed Brannan had been born and raised in America, but she knew he'd picked it up from Kernaghan, who'd been raised in the old country. "Why rehash all that teenage heavy breathing at this point, Brannan?" she asked, pointedly looking at his hand on her arm.

"Heavy breathing? Is that what you call it, Kelly Flynn? You reduce what we felt, what we had, to heavy breathing?" He grabbed her other arm and lifted her up to the step where he was standing.

"Quit moving me around like I'm some kind of cardboard movie prop," Kelly protested, trying without success to wriggle out of his grasp.

"I'll move you all right," he said, then without warning lowered his head to capture her lips in a kiss so fierce and possessive, Kelly was instantly intoxicated, instantly deprived of any willpower she may have had to resist him. She made one feeble attempt to push him away, but she might as well have been pushing on a steep granite cliff. Inexorably her body was drawn against his as his hands roamed greedily over her, molding her soft curves to his unyielding frame. His lips crushed hers, then grew gentle and tentative, while his tongue dipped into her mouth. He tasted her, then eagerly devoured her, like a man who'd been hungry for too long.

Kelly's arms slid around Jed's neck, all thought of resistance banished as she gave herself up to the delicious ecstasy only he could give her. Her tongue danced with his, and the greater the demands of his lips the softer and more giving hers became. As his hands stroked her back and pressed on the base of her spine to make her feel the heat and hardness of him, her breasts grew swollen with desire, aching to be cupped in his palms.

It happened again. Jed pulled away, leaving Kelly gasping with the need he'd created, her head tipped back and her eyes half closed, her body too weak to stand on its own. He held her while she tried to catch her breath, but he continued his sensual attack. Though his lips had abandoned hers and his chest was no longer there for her to lean on, he kept his hand on the base of her spine, pressing her against him. "Are you old enough yet," he said in a strained voice, "to know when a man wants you so much he's half crazy from it? Are you mature enough to understand what he has to go through to stop himself from taking you? Or can you feel what's happening, what effect you have, and still think it was easy for me?"

Kelly tried to drag herself away, but Jed only allowed her to move enough to stimulate them both even more. She thought her body would explode with need. Opening her eyes she was shocked to see the clear blue sky of morning instead of the starry black velvet sky of night. It snapped her to her senses. "We're not on a beach now, we're right out in public!" The protest sounded lame even to her; a moment ago she hadn't cared where they were.

Jed didn't bother pointing that out. He just continued tormenting her with the promise of his body—and tormenting himself as well. "I love the way you respond to me, Kelly," he whispered. "That flush that's spreading over your throat and face . . . I remember now it starts on the swelling of your breasts and moves upwards . . ."

Kelly moaned. "Oh, please."

He was relentless. "Please," he repeated. "You used to

add my name to that. 'Please, Jed,' you'd cry out. 'Please, Jed, don't stop. Please Jed, love me.' Lord, I used to die a thousand times forcing myself to pull away and see your tears of frustration and longing. Maybe I was wrong. Maybe I should have made you all mine, Kelly. It could have changed so much of what happened."

"It's academic, Brannan," Kelly managed to fling back at him. "You did pull away. You did stop. You didn't love me, and I don't know why you want to repeat the whole sorry business now. You left me seven years ago. I got over you. It wasn't easy, but I did it. So don't do this to me now." Her voice broke on a sob. "Wasn't it enough to tear me apart once?"

Her words pierced Jed's heart. "I did love you, Kelly," he said in a low voice. "I didn't want to tear you apart then, and I'm not going to do it now."

"So what do you want?" Kelly cried.

Jed moved his hands upward over her back in long, soothing strokes, gathering her into the cradle of his body. "I want to love you, Kelly. There'll be no stopping this time around. And I want you to quit calling me 'Brannan.' A wife should call her husband by his first name, don't you think?" He grazed his lips over her ear and told her the simple, bold truth. "And I do intend, girl, to marry you."

Three

Kelly's thoughts whirled in her mind like the symbols of a slot machine. She closed her eyes, hoping some logical pattern would emerge from the confused images. Reality was blurred; it mingled with the dreams she'd never been able to banish. Were Jed Brannan's lips brushing hers as he murmured soft and persuasive words, or was it simply another fantasy? His fingers seemed to be caressing her cheeks with heart catching tenderness, but was it actually happening? She couldn't be as weightless as she felt, floating blissfully on a cloud of sensuality. She wasn't a winged creature bursting forth from a tight cocoon. Dreams, they were only dreams.

Jed's lips trailed downward along a pulsating cord of her throat, reawakening her skin's nerve endings to remembered pleasure. Instinctively she tilted back her head to give him access to the sensitive area just under her chin.

His hands drifted to her shoulders, massaging them, while his thumbs drew ever-widening arcs that flirted at the inside edges of her suit lapels until the gentle slopes of her breasts grew swollen, reaching toward his touch, the nipples engorged and thrusting against the cool silk of her blouse.

Kelly heard a soft moan and knew it had escaped from her own parted lips. She wondered if Jed was aware of the helpless sound. Could fantasy characters hear?

With tentative fingers, Kelly explored the contours of his face, learning anew the high cheekbones, the thick brows, the straight nose with its unfamiliar bump. He drew a delicate line of kisses to her earlobe, then nibbled at a spot that sent erotic shocks all the way down to her inner thighs. She gasped, loving the strength of his rough-hewn features. He wasn't a fantasy. He wasn't a dream. No dream man could arouse her to heights of need this way.

Jed was real and he was there, caressing her, kissing her, wanting her. Impossible as it seemed, he even wanted to marry her. No, *intended* to marry her.

A pattern finally clicked into place. Kelly's eyes snapped open. "You *intend* to marry me? *Intend?* Is that what you said, Brannan?"

Jed froze. He knew he'd made a mistake and wasn't sure how to get out of it. He'd said it, all right. *Intend.* He couldn't believe he'd been such an idiot.

Kelly shook herself free of him and stepped backward. "Listen up, mister." Her voice was low and shaky as she tried to fight desire Jed had awakened in her. "I wouldn't know how a wife should address her husband, Brannan, but in your case any name with more than four letters is a compliment you don't deserve."

Jed took a step toward her and grasped her shoulders. "Kelly, I didn't mean . . ."

"In any event," she went on, her voice rising with indignation, "the question doesn't concern me, because I don't *intend* to be a wife—most particularly *your* wife. In case you haven't noticed, your intention isn't enough. Unless the rules have been changed lately, it takes two to dance that jig."

"Tango," Jed put in lamely in the wild hope he could stem with idle chatter the tide of her burgeoning rage. "Two to tango."

"I'll choose my own dances," Kelly shot back. "And my own partners. And let me tell you one more thing, you . . . you . . . Celtic Casanova. No man kisses Kelly Flynn until she asks for it, understand?" She brought up her arms in an abrupt move that knocked his hands off her shoulders, and then she dashed down the steps.

Jed caught up as she reached the walk. He whirled her around to face him. "Kelly Flynn asks for it," he told her, his own voice shaking now. He was mad and he was worried. He couldn't lose her over such a stupid slip of the tongue! She'd responded with even more fire than he remembered she possessed. "Kelly Flynn asks for it," he said again, pinning her green eyes with his determined gaze. "She asks for it every time she looks at me."

"She does no such thing!" Kelly shouted, long past caring whether the neighbors heard or saw the show they were putting on. She struggled to get away from Jed, but his grip on her upper arms was unbreakable. "That's just your overblown male ego causing you to see what you want to see!"

Jed's eyes narrowed. "It's no use lying to me, Kelly, even if you insist on lying to yourself. I know you too well. And overblown male ego or not, I can see very clearly what's going on in those green eyes of yours. They're deep, limpid pools of—"

"Deep limpid pools?" she cried, then forced a mocking laugh. "Deep limpid pools! You'd better head for the Emerald Isle and a smooch with the Blarney stone if that's the best you can do, Brannan. At least my garbled clichés are original!" Desperate to escape before he weakened her defenses again, Kelly tried flattening her palms on his chest and pushing with all her might.

The wall of male sinew and muscle didn't budge, but to her surprise, the force of her action sent her flying back, loosening Jed's hold.

His eyes widened. "Kelly!" He tried to catch her, but her flailing arms got in the way and he held his breath, terrified. Somehow she managed to get her balance and land on her feet, still upright, and though Jed sighed with relief, he wanted to throttle her. She could have hurt herself! "It'd serve you right if you'd fallen flat on your pretty little keister!" he shouted, moving toward her.

Kelly made a run for her car, jumped inside and locked the door, then rolled down the window. "I should have landed a right hook to your eager little kisser, Brannan! That's what I should have done!"

Suddenly aware that his carefully orchestrated plan to woo Kelly had degenerated from romance to low comedy, Jed couldn't help laughing. "Mighty Mite," he said, shaking his head. "You're the same bratty shrimp you always were. You think you're so tough."

Kelly switched on the ignition and, ready for a fast getaway, conceded the point. "Right," she agreed. "Gidget with a John Wayne complex, that's me."

Jed tilted back his head and laughed harder as a burst of renewed affection for this impossible female permeated his whole being.

Kelly gave a little sniff, checked the driveway behind her, and carefully backed the car out onto the street. No matter how upset she was, she refused to vent her anger on her car. Besides, the last thing she needed was an accident, especially with a smug male watching. She switched into first gear and concentrated on driving away from the scene of her most stupid act since she'd fallen for Jed Brannan the first time.

Halfway down the block she glanced in the rearview mirror and saw Jed on the sidewalk watching her, his hands resting loosely on his lean hips, his mouth still curved in a crooked grin.

She gave in to an impulse to honk at him and immediately regretted it. The sound was a perky greeting, not a blast of defiance. Detroit car manufacturers had taken all the spunk out of car horns.

When Jed responded with a cheerful, cavalier wave, Kelly swore. He was so sure of himself, so sure of her. All right, she'd given him some reason for his overconfidence, but it wouldn't happen again. Jed Brannan was a pirate who thought nothing of cutting out a woman's heart and tossing it to the dogs, but she was older and smarter now.

The thought nagged at her that she might be overreacting to the situation, perhaps even being a trifle melodramatic. She had to admit she had the tendency to do so, especially when a particular man was involved. He made her lose all sense of proportion. He stirred up her libido and her temper, when she wanted only peace. He drove her crazy!

As Kelly turned the corner at the end of the street, Jed gave her one last wave, his smile fading. He was shocked by the sudden bleakness of his mood. What if this was no joke? What if his blunder had finished his chances with Kelly?

He glanced at the apple tree at the corner of the house, at the sloping lawn, at the plump shrubbery nestled below the porch. Kelly's power over him was awesome, he realized, letting his gaze sweep upward to the hanging pots of pansies and petunias, the window boxes of geraniums. With her around, his world had a special glow. It was Technicolor. Hell, it was living color. When she was gone it was as if he were in a colorized version of an old movie.

Shoving his hands into his pockets, he walked up the front walk, head down, shoulders slumped. He kicked at a stone and sighed. Had he blown everything? Surely not. Kelly wouldn't have melted in his arms the way she did unless she felt something for him. No matter how angry she was at his stupid show of arrogance, she had to come around eventually. It wasn't that he considered himself irresistible—not in general, anyway. He simply believed he was irresistible to *her*, and that was only because he was utterly convinced they were meant for each other. If they weren't, why hadn't either of them found someone else in all this time? Kelly had gone with a couple of guys in college, but those romances had ended. Her engagement had sent him into a tailspin when he'd heard about it, but it had ended as well. And according to Kernaghan, she'd hardly dated for nearly three years. It wasn't natural for a pretty girl her age not to date. It only made sense if it was because she knew damn well who she really belonged with.

Jed knew who he belonged with too. He'd tried hard enough to get over Kelly. When she'd ignored all his early letters, he'd worked, really worked at forgetting her. After a few months he'd managed to banish her from most of his waking thoughts. Only his nights had been haunted by the vision of the hurt in her eyes when he'd told her he was leaving, when he'd said, trying to be fair and mature and reasonable, that she should date other people while he was gone, that she was too young to be tied down. What he'd done as an act of truly selfless love, she'd interpreted as betrayal.

When he'd gotten word she was at college studying art and displaying real talent, he'd told himself his decision to let her go was the right one. Even the news that she was seeing someone seriously had helped him move on to plan his life without Kelly Flynn . . . or so he'd told himself.

But all the time he'd just been submerging his emotions, pushing them down and down. He'd been like a river frozen over, his feelings trapped under a sheet of ice, yet still flowing, churning, pushing at the surface. Now it was time for the spring thaw. Now that he'd seen Kelly again, now that he'd held her and kissed her and experienced the transformation of a girl's desire to a woman's passion, a torrent of need was bubbling up inside him, bursting free.

He bounded up the front steps and threw himself onto the porch swing, all at once engulfed by an insane impulse to run down the street after Kelly, drag her out of her car, and carry her back here for keeps. Maybe he *was* an arrogant, overbearing Irishman. He smiled at the thought. His urge to steamroll right over Kelly's protests was stupid, primitive . . . and almost irresistible. Would she really mind so much? She was afraid. That was why she'd gone tearing off in one of her fine tempers. She was terrified. Maybe it was up to him to conquer her fear for her, to force—

The front door opened and Jed glanced up. Dorothy was standing behind the screen. She was giving him one of her serious looks.

Guiltily, he slowed the rhythm of his rocking, suddenly aware how the swing had shrieked when he'd landed on it, and how it was creaking and groaning now.

"You'll break that swing yet," Dorothy chided, just as she'd scolded him all his life. She stepped out onto the porch, her hands on her hips. "You can't just *ride* it, you know. It's not that old hobby horse you abused when you were little. And come to think of it, you broke *that* before you were six. Things can't stand up to your rough ways, Jed."

He pondered those words. Was Dorothy really talking about the porch swing or had she read his thoughts about wooing Kelly Neanderthal-style? "Neither can people," he muttered at last, jumping up to pace back and forth, powered by an excess of nervous energy.

Dorothy's lips quirked in a smile. "What's wrong?" she asked him. "Didn't Kelly let you sweep her off her feet? Did you go too fast for her?"

Jed stopped in his tracks and stared at the woman. He hadn't even told her he wanted to win Kelly back. He hadn't told anyone. Was he that transparent? She was right, however, he realized. He'd gone much too fast. Worse, he hadn't learned from his mistake. He'd actually been sitting here thinking about going even faster. "Something like that," he admitted finally.

"Give her time," Dorothy suggested sympathetically. "Kelly isn't one of your fawning playmates, remember. She's her own person. But she does care for you, Jed."

Jed made an unintelligible sound.

"Another of your lovers' quarrels?" the housekeeper asked. "There was a lot of shouting going on out here."

"If I'd been standing in the driveway," Jed answered. "Kelly would have run me down—and cheered while she was doing it. For a minute I thought she'd drive across the lawn to get me."

"She really shouldn't drive when she's upset," Dorothy remarked, brushing back a stray hair that had come loose from the bun at the nape of her neck.

Jed rose to Kelly's defense. "She was careful. Anyway, I know her. She'll park a couple of blocks away and cool off. Kelly doesn't take stupid chances."

Dorothy shook her head and chuckled quietly. "As I said to Kelly when she arrived, some things never change. You'll shout at her yourself, but Lord help anyone else who so much as looks sideways at the girl." The strong lines of the older woman's face softened. "You never stopped loving Kelly, did you?"

"Never," Jed admitted. It wasn't something he was ashamed of, but he felt silly about it. "Kelly says I'm corny," he added.

"You're not corny. You're a swan."

Jed cocked his head to one side and frowned. "A swan," he repeated, puzzled.

Dorothy nodded complacently. "A swan is faithful to one mate for life. Now, given the Barbie dolls I've watched you waste your time on, I can't say you've been totally faithful, but there's never really been anyone for you but Kelly, so you're a swan. She's lucky. Swans are rare."

Jed put his arm around Dorothy's shoulders. "At the moment I believe my intended mate thinks of me more as an ugly duckling than a swan."

"More likely a rooster," Dorothy retorted. "A strutting rooster. You've been spoiled by females all your life, Jed Brannan, your mother and myself included. Your cocky ways won't go over well with Kelly Flynn, let me warn you."

"Swans, mynah birds, roosters," Jed grumbled. Dorothy knew him too well. She was too close to the mark with her observations. "Whichever I am," he said with a wink and a grin, "I'll win Kelly by means fair or fowl."

Dorothy groaned and made a face. "Kelly's right. You're corny. Just like Kernaghan."

Jed's spirits lifted. Just like Kernaghan? Maybe he wasn't such a hopeless case after all.

"I came out to call you to lunch," Dorothy said, interrupting his thoughts of how Kernaghan would court Kelly Flynn.

"Lunch?" he repeated, as if the concept were something new to him.

"That is, if you're not so lovesick that you've lost your appetite."

Jed opened the screen door and waved Dorothy inside the house ahead of him. "If lovesickness destroyed my appetite," he said truthfully, "I'd be long dead."

Four blocks away Kelly was parked on the side of a quiet street waiting for her violent trembling to subside. Residential streets she could manage, but she wasn't about to brave the tourist-swollen main arteries downtown until she'd regained control of herself.

She concentrated hard on breathing slowly, deeply. If women giving birth could manage their pain this way, she could use the same technique for overruling her racing pulse and pounding heart. She wouldn't even think about Jed Brannan, not for a single second.

The nerve of him, expecting her to fall at his feet because he was ready to waltz back and fill up her dance card. Well, her dance card already happened to be full. Not with men, maybe, but with . . . other things—work, friends. A few friends. A couple. Kelly frowned. She didn't have very many friends now that she thought about it, unless she counted the people she worked with, such as buyers and seamstresses and the artisans who did her stained-glass work. There'd been no time for socializing. Maybe she ought to do more of that sort of thing so she wouldn't be so vulnerable to Jed Brannan.

Dear Lord, she thought, leaning her head against the seat and rubbing her eyes with her thumb and forefinger. His kisses. They seared her skin and fanned into open flames the dormant embers of her desire.

She remembered she wasn't supposed to be thinking of him. She was supposed to be breathing. *Inhale, two, three, four,* she counted. *Exhale . . .* But really, Jed was so arrogant it was impossible not to think about him! Coaxing her into accepting the assignment to do the portrait of Beauregarde, then trying to seduce her right in the front yard.

Back to the breathing, she reminded herself. Instead of cooling off she was heating up. *Inhale, two, three . . .* Jed Brannan wasn't going to have this power over her, no way. *Inhale—no, exhale . . .*

She raised her head and cursed through clenched teeth. He'd gotten to her. He'd made her want him with an ache that wouldn't go away. He'd made her remember what she'd forced herself to forget—the sweet, minty taste of his lips, the palpable waves of heat emanating from his body, the prefect comfort of his arms. It wasn't fair. He could have any woman he wanted. Why did he choose to torment her?

Why had she let herself be talked into doing that portrait? She couldn't bear to face Jed again, couldn't take the chance that he'd reduce her to the uncontrollable state she'd been in today.

She had to do the portrait, she realized, because to ignore Kernaghan's last request was unthinkable.

Jed worked from his house, so he was always around. It would be impossible to snap Beauregarde's picture without running into the bird's new master. Which, she knew, was exactly what Jed was counting on.

After she'd sat thinking for several more minutes, an idea hit her. The tennis club. She was a member, but rarely had time to play. Nevertheless, she often went to the club dining room for business lunches, and she'd seen Jed's name on the tournament rosters on the bulletin board.

All she had to do was check the rosters, wait until Jed was involved in a tournament, then call his secretary and arrange to zip right over and take the picture of the mynah bird. There was no need whatsover to meet with him again. Now if she could just figure out how to run him out of town, her life would be complete. She was as determined to avoid him as if he were going to serve her with a summons. Or give her measles. Or hit her up for a loan.

Or kiss her until she forgot who she was, she admitted with a sinking heart. Why had he gotten more gorgeous, more exciting than ever? He had no right! Rotten Irishman.

Calm at last, Kelly started the car and drove downtown to visit a boutique that carried her gift line. Shamrock Specialties had blossomed into a huge, unexpected success in the past two years. Its logo had evidently brought her good luck.

She couldn't help smiling; Jed must find it puzzling that she called him an Irishman as an insult. She'd done it years ago for the first time, and though he'd cocked his head to one side in that way he had of looking adorably confused, she remembered, he'd never made much of the fact that the epithet didn't make sense. In truth, Kelly's ancestry was more pure Irish than Jed's. He'd had an English grandmother.

Her sixteenth birthday, she recalled as she drove. It was the first time she'd quarreled with Jed and the beginning, in a way, of their romance.

Kernaghan had thrown a big party for her, complete with streamers and balloons and Japanese lanterns. Kelly's crush on Jed had developed the previous summer and had intensified when he'd arrived in town before her birthday in late May.

Kelly had felt quite grown-up, almost glamorous. Her white eyelet sundress was new, her long brown hair cut in a style that was a perfect copy of Farrah Fawcett's windblown look. Surely Jed would notice her as a woman, not just the adolescent daughter of Kernaghan's friends.

But she'd been relegated to the soda-pop-and-cookies crowd, expected to play hostess to a bunch of teenagers dancing to rock music in the basement, while Jed was part of the adult gathering, sipping cocktails and nibbling hors d'oeuvres in the living room.

The summer night had lured couples outside to steal a few kisses in the shadows of the leafy trees in the yard. Kelly, bored with the antics of children, had gone for a walk.

Kelly had spied Jed smiling down at the most beautiful girl she'd ever seen, her hair pale gold in the moonlight, her eyes luminous as she gazed up at Jed, her full lips waiting for his kiss. She hadn't waited long.

Kelly still remembered vividly the abject misery she'd felt at that moment. She should have known then that Jed Brannan had the power to make her absolutely miserable.

Well, she knew now.

Reaching the downtown area, she looked for a parking spot near the boutique. When she saw one, she maneuvered her car into it, turned off the ignition, and dug into her purse for a coin.

While she was putting the coin in the meter, she caught an unexpected reflection of herself in a store window. She hated when that happened. Somehow she managed to envision herself as being much taller and more voluptuous, and it always shocked her to be faced with the truth.

She'd felt the same way on the night of her birthday party, after seeing Jed kiss another woman.

Suddenly the white eyelet dress had seemed babyish and the Farrah Fawcett hairdo dated. And her figure? Kelly had looked down at herself then, as she did now, and thought, "What figure?" At twenty-five it didn't seem so important, but at sixteen her modest proportions had constituted a disaster.

She'd taken her first drink that night, getting away with it because no one had paid much attention when she'd joined the party in the living room, smiling bravely though her heart was broken. Making her way to the self-serve bar she'd helped herself to a generous dollop of Irish whiskey, determined to drown her sorrows in a life of dissipation if she couldn't hope to attract Jed Brannan, if she couldn't hope he would kiss her the way he'd kissed . . . Miss Universe.

It was no wonder she wasn't a drinker, Kelly thought as she walked toward the boutique. She could choke even now at the thought of the way that whiskey had burned.

She'd forced it down, though. In fact, she was pouring a second glass when Jed and his lady love had walked back into the house.

Jed had spotted Kelly's mischief instantly. He'd been kind enough not to make a scene. He'd excused himself from his girl, stalked purposefully to Kelly, and taken the glass right out of her hand. "Straight Irish whiskey?" he'd remarked. "You've decided to celebrate by becoming a lush?"

"What's it to you, Romeo?" she'd answered.

"I don't believe my grandfather threw this party for a little girl who'd filch his whiskey."

"I'm not a little girl. I'm sixteen. People get married at sixteen."

"And regret it before they're seventeen. Now what would you really like to drink, Kelly? I'll do the honors."

"Vodka," she'd said sweetly.

"Try again."

"Scotch."

"Lemon soda, you say? Of course." Curling his fingers around her wrist, he'd practically dragged her out to the kitchen. "Come with me, birthday girl. We'll get you a cold one from the fridge." As soon as they were alone he'd pushed her into a corner and started his lecture.

"What kind of trick were you going to pull?" he'd demanded. "Kernaghan throws a party in your honor, and you thank him by trying to get drunk. You should be ashamed, Kelly. That man thinks you're an angel."

Kelly, uncomfortably aware that Jed was right, had reacted with fury. "Mind your own business, Jed Brannan. Go back outside and take up your cheap necking where you left off! Don't try to tell me what I can and can't drink. You're not my boss, you know. You're just a big show-off. A playboy. A . . . a . . . a damned Irishman!"

All these years later Kelly couldn't figure out why she'd said that, but once she'd uttered the words she couldn't back down. She'd done the same thing in her last encounter with Jed. Her only satisfaction the first time had been seeing Jed's jaw drop in shock. Girls didn't talk to him that way. He'd been speechless.

His silence hadn't lasted long, however. He'd made several threats dire enough to persuade Kelly that lemon soda was pretty refreshing after all. And Jed had kept an eye on her for the rest of the evening. She hadn't minded one bit.

Miss Universe hadn't been too pleased. Miss Universe had gone home in a snit, but Jed hadn't appeared to notice.

Thus the romance began, Kelly thought with a nostalgic sigh. Love had blossomed slowly at first because of their age difference, but it had bloomed exuberantly after her eighteenth birthday—only to wilt before her nineteenth. Faced with a choice between love and adventure, Jed had chosen adventure. He'd gone away.

"He should have stayed away,' she muttered under her breath. He didn't need Traverse City, and Traverse City certainly didn't need him. She swung open the boutique door and strode inside.

Two hours later she left with a huge order. Her only

problem now was figuring out how she was going to meet the delivery date.

As she climbed into her car she grinned. This was her favorite kind of problem. Her least favorite was an empty order form. Success felt good—it felt great. When she realized she'd hardly given Jed Brannan a thought during the whole session with the boutique's buyer, her grin widened. Work had accomplished what will-power failed to do: It had kept her mind off taboo subjects.

Work always did that for her, she mused as she buckled her seat belt and started the car. It was more than her livelihood, even more than her vocation. It was therapy, a kind of oblivion. It was her salvation.

She drove to her next appointment, confident she'd rediscovered the key to her self-control. Jed Brannan, she told herself in a burst of triumph, was once again in the past.

Four

It was Saturday morning. Six days had passed and Kelly still hadn't called Diane to arrange to take a picture of Beauregarde. Jed was trying to be patient, but he wasn't a patient man by nature. And it began to nag at him that he'd never accomplished or won anything he cared about by sitting back and waiting for it to come to him. Why should Kelly be any different?

He decided to give her one more day to make it a full week. Then if he hadn't heard from her, she'd hear from him. It was as simple as that.

After he made his decision, he felt better. So much better, he trounced all opponents in the tennis tournament at the club. Singles, doubles, mixed doubles . . . he played every kind of match possible, and nobody could beat him.

A winning streak, he told himself on the way home at five o'clock. Now, if it would just hold out and work for more important matters . . .

"Hi." Dorothy greeted him as he bounded into the house. "You did well today, then."

Jed laughed. "Was it on TV or are you reading my mind again?"

"Reading your walk," she answered. "There's a certain jauntiness to your step when things have gone well for you. You act just like your grandfather."

Just like Kernaghan again, Jed thought. He really was on a winning streak. "So what's happening around here?" he asked, grabbing an apple and biting into it.

"Not much. Oh, Kelly dropped in to take a snapshot of Beauregarde."

Jed's teeth remained embedded in the apple as he stared at Dorothy. So much for his winning streak, he thought. He bit through the fruit, chewing quickly as he tried to figure out how Kelly had managed to put one over on him. "Diane wasn't working today," he said, thinking out loud. "Kelly was supposed to call first to arrange an appointment. She couldn't have done it. Diane wasn't here."

"Well I was here, Jed. She called me," Dorothy pointed out as she calmly kneaded a mound of bread dough.

"She was supposed to make arrangements in advance."

"She said she had an appointment in the neighborhood and it would really help her meet her schedule if she could stop here at the same time." The housekeeper slapped the bread dough into a pan to rise and washed her hands, turning to smile at Jed as she dried them. "So in courtship you're not doing quite as well as on the court it appears. In this match the score is fifteen for Kelly, love for Jed."

Jed demolished his apple, tossed the core in the garbage, and wiped his hands on his tennis shorts. "The little . . ."

"She's a worthy opponent," Dorothy remarked. "You have to grant her that."

"She's not supposed to be an opponent," Jed ground out through clenched teeth.

"That's your opinion. Obviously hers is different."

"Fine," Jed said, narrowing his eyes as he stared off into space, adjusting his plans. "Just fine. But don't get too caught up in cheering her on, because this match has just started. Hell, the first game has barely begun. It's my serve now."

"I'm looking forward to this tournament," Dorothy teased. "I've always relished a hotly contested battle."

"Whose side are you on, anyway?' he demanded, grabbing four cookies off a plate.

Dorothy reached out and removed three of the cookies from his hand. "Your dinner's nearly ready. And I'm on your side. Also Kelly's."

Jed watched her put the cookies down, then simply took them again. There were times when a man had to assert himself.

"You're incorrigible," Dorothy chided with a laugh.

He stalked toward the staircase to go upstairs and shower. "I plan to be, let me tell you. The hell with patience."

In her cottage on the beach, Kelly stood beside her desk and stared at her answering machine with such revulsion it might have been a coiled poisonous reptile.

State-of-the-art perversion, she thought as she gave the machine's dial a vicious twist to rewind the tape. Usually she allowed incoming calls to be recorded over the old ones, but she decided to erase this tape completely before resetting it. To leave it would be as bad as neglecting to scrub pornographic graffiti off the walls.

She marched into her bedroom, wondering what to do about the problem. It was infuriating. For every wonderful innovation there seemed to be an endless supply of creeps to exploit and ruin it. Nowadays the anonymous bullies who got their thrills terrorizing women by telephone had a new convenience. All they had to do was punch out numbers at random, and eventually a recorded greeting would supply a name and often other vital data. Then, at the sound of a tone, the answering machine would helpfully preserve a filthy message to be delivered when the unsuspecting victim came home.

Every single day for two weeks Kelly had been harassed by a man with a thin, singsong voice, and she was getting thoroughly tired of it. But she wouldn't let herself be terrorized. These characters were cowards. Anonymous callers didn't have the nerve to come out into the open.

She'd thought of getting an unlisted number, but it would play havoc with her business. No sly, insinuating, disembodied voice was going to drive her to such lengths, even if she got a call every day for the next year.

The only concession she made to the nuisance was to see that all her doors and windows were locked after dark. She resented having to go that far, because the hot weather had arrived and she was sweltering instead of enjoying the cool breezes that skimmed over Lake Michigan and straight into her little house. Accustomed to sleeping with the window open she'd begun waking up in the morning with a headache due to the lack of fresh air.

She stripped off her clothes, enjoying the freedom of near nakedness for a moment, then pulled on a pair of electric-blue shorts over her cotton bikini panties. Leaving off her bra, she slipped into a Hawaiian-floral blouse, fastening only a couple of the middle buttons and tying the shirttails under her breast.

As she slid her bare feet into yellow sandals, she grabbed an elastic from a dish on the dresser, then walked back into the kitchen, pulling her hair up into a loose topknot.

Dinner, she decided, and hoped there was some kind

of boil-in-a-bag meal in the freezer. She didn't want to turn on the oven to bake frozen lasagna, and she didn't have a microwave, so she was faced with either a boil-in-a-bag meal or a tomato sandwich. Kelly was always vowing to cook proper meals for herself, but she never seemed to get around to it. She rarely even found the time or energy to buy enough groceries.

One of the great things about living alone, she mused, was that she would eat when and what she wanted. No man sat enthroned within her little castle, waiting behind a newspaper for mesquite-grilled chicken and homemade pasta.

The icy air that blasted out at her from inside the freezer was wonderful, but she was out of luck on finding something to eat. A tomato sandwich it would be, Kelly thought, not really caring.

She was prying two slices of bread from the loaf in the freezer when a knock at the door gave her such a start, she yelped and leaped straight up, hitting her head on the roof of the fridge. Both bread slices flew across the room, landing on the floor and skittering across the tile and halfway under the stove.

Possibly, she thought as she rubbed her head, those stupid phone calls had made her a bit skittish.

She retrieved the bread and threw it in the garbage on her way to the door.

At the front door she stopped abruptly. It was still early evening and not dark out, but did she really want to open the door with no idea who was out there? What if her theory about anonymous callers was all wet?

Another knock, this one sharper, jarred her into action. She took a step forward, then stopped again. Why hadn't she gotten around to installing a peephole? And why didn't she keep the radio or television playing so it wouldn't be obvious that she was alone? she asked herself. If she hadn't made so much noise when she'd heard the knock, she could pretend not to be home.

"Kelly?" a familiar voice called. "It's Jed."

She was too shocked and relieved to think clearly, and she had the door wide open before she remembered that the man was as dangerous to her in his own way as any strangler.

She realized she'd made a serious mistake the second she saw him. His steel-gray, lightweight suit fit perfectly and the color served to intensify the smoky darkness of his eyes. A remarkably masculine pink shirt cast a glow over Jed's golden skin, highlighting the hard, rugged planes of his features. "You're wearing a tie," Kelly murmured, taking in the muted pewter-and-rose striped silk instead of allowing her gaze to travel from his wide shoulders to his narrow waist and lean hips.

"I do sometimes," he answered, smiling down at her. Jed had rehearsed several possible scenarios on the way to Kelly's house. None of them included a discussion of his tie.

"You never used to wear them," she said in a soft voice, swallowing hard. He was more beautiful every time she saw him. It was rotten of him.

"I used to wear them," Jed argued, bemused by Kelly's obvious discomfort. "For special occasions, anyway. And that's why I wear them now—for special occasions." *Ask me*, he pleaded silently. *Give me a cue line, here. Ask me what special occasion this is.*

Kelly didn't. She chewed on her lower lip, torn between slamming the door in his face and flying into his arms.

"This is a special occasion," Jed said at last, giving up on Kelly.

She blinked, then looked at him as if she'd just realized what he'd said. "I beg your pardon?"

"I said that this is a special occasion, Kelly."

"Are you on your way to the tennis club dance?" she asked, trying not to give in to the feelings the thought aroused in her.

"Oh, you're aware of the dance, are you?"

"Well I *am* a member of the club, even if I haven't spent a lot of time there lately," Kelly replied, all at once aware of the skimpiness of her outfit. Jed's gaze, traveling slowly over her as he spoke, made her feel completely naked . . . and what bothered her most was that it wasn't an unpleasant sensation. She folded her arms over her bare midriff and stepped back, inclining her head to indicate that he could come all the way into the house.

"I guess members get notices of tournaments," he remarked, his eyes twinkling as he followed her.

So he knew, Kelly thought. He knew she'd taken Beau's picture while he was occupied on the courts. "Was there a tournament?" she asked with feigned innocence.

Jed refused to let her get away with it. "Why so scared of me, Kelly?"

"Scared? You think I'm scared of you, Brannan?" Somehow Kelly didn't feel she was putting enough defiance into her voice.

"Why else would you contrive to take that snapshot while I was out of the house?"

"Oh, that," Kelly said, turning to walk away from Jed and head toward a chair in the living room.

"That," Jed repeated. He grinned, enjoying the view Kelly presented in her short-shorts. He'd always loved her legs, their slender lines so perfectly shaped and proportioned. The years had been more than kind to the saucy curve of her bottom; Jed clenched his hands into tight fists to restrain himself from grabbing her and pressing his fingers into the firm, ripe mounds.

Kelly settled into an overstuffed chair and tucked her

legs up under her, keeping her arms folded. "It was simply a convenient opportunity for me to take Beau's picture today. I was in the neighborhood. Why should I be afraid of you?"

Jed walked slowly toward her. "That's what I was asking," he pointed out. "Why *are* you afraid?"

"I'm not. As usual, your ego is making you read dark meanings into the simplest of events. I had no idea you were playing in that tournament today and wouldn't—" She stopped, realizing what she'd said.

"Wouldn't be at home," Jed supplied. He crouched in front of her so his eyes were level with hers. "In any case, I'm glad you've started the job. Did Beau treat you decently?"

Kelly had to smile, though Jed's proximity and his penetrating gaze made her light-headed. "He called me 'chickie,' actually. A *bird* called me 'chickie'!"

Jed chuckled. "I warned you. Kernaghan taught him some bad habits."

"I can't believe it was Kernaghan. It was probably your doing."

"Not mine. I wouldn't have the patience to teach that bird anything. Did he sing for you?"

Kelly rolled her eyes, then nearly jumped out of her skin as Jed calmly, casually, destroyed the shield she made with her folded arms by clasping one of her hands between his. She forced herself to keep up the banter. "I suppose you want me to believe that Beauregarde sings *Carmen* or *Tosca*."

"Nothing so grand," Jed answered, turning Kelly's palm upward and tracing its lines with his index finger. "Just 'True Love.' Beau's repertoire is romantic but limited."

Kelly wanted to pull her hand away, but her brain wouldn't give the command; she was lulled into a half-stupor by Jed's light, tantalizing caress. "Taking up palm reading?" she managed to ask in a small voice.

His lips curved in a smile and he nodded. Now she was playing her part, albeit unwittingly . . . and unwillingly. With a nod he brought her hand up closer to his face so he could study it. "Mmm," he murmured, "I'm new at it, though. I can only read the immediate future. Take yours, for instance. I see . . ." He hesitated, frowning, pretending to concentrate. "Only the next couple of hours," he said at last. "I see a . . . a celebration of some kind. Tables in a fine restaurant. Candlelight." He peered more closely at her palm. What he actually saw was that Kelly's hand was trembling, but he didn't bother to point that out. "You're with a man, sipping champagne, laughing . . . there's music in the background."

"Beauregarde singing 'True Love,' no doubt," Kelly said. "And what's the celebration? Has Jed Brannan been called out of town? Permanently, perhaps?"

"Let me check," he replied, determined to use her jibes to his own advantage. He looked up from his contemplation of her palm to capture and hold her gaze with his as he brought her hand to his lips. "I'm an unconventional sort of mystic," he said softly, grazing his mouth over the tender inside of her wrist. "I approach the puzzle from various perspectives."

Kelly couldn't suppress the urge to take in a sudden breath as Jed trailed the tip of his tongue over her palm. She wasn't sure how accurate his fortune-telling was, but she'd have sworn he'd gone straight to her love line. Her whole body quivered with searing desire.

Jed heard her gasp and saw the vein in her wrist pulsating wildly. The score was even, he decided. Kelly fifteen, Jed fifteen. Now he had to press for the lead. "Yes," he whispered. "It's coming through clearly now.

Jed Brannan hasn't been called out of town permanently. Not at all. Jed Brannan is the man with you in the restaurant. The celebration is . . ." He hesitated, gently nibbling on her finger and then swirling his tongue around its delicate tip. "That's it," he said when Kelly's eyes closed and she gave another helpless gasp. "The celebration is to mark the honoring of a good man's last request." Jed didn't feel the slightest bit guilty about using Kernaghan; his grandfather would have done the same. Kelly's response to what he was doing to her finger was intriguing. Perhaps he'd try another move. The score was now Kelly fifteen, Jed thirty.

Unaware that she was one of many opponents who'd gone down to defeat before Jed Brannan today, Kelly was involved in a struggle of her own, a battle against the engulfing waves of excitement that washed over her. Jed's lips and tongue explored the intensely erotic potential of palm reading, adding touches she dimly thought were his own invention, or perhaps masterful techniques he'd learned in some exotic country. She reveled in the delicious sensations, then fought the current that was carrying her to strange and unfamiliar regions, then gave in to them again, too blissful to care what shores she landed on.

Jed watched a pink flush spread over her throat and changed his score to forty. When Kelly's free hand reached out to stroke his hair and trace the contours of his face, he awarded himself the game. It was the sweetest victory of his life. "Kelly-love," he murmured, resurrecting the name he'd called her so long ago. With every evidence of her response, he felt his own body swelling with an urgent demand. He'd played his game for a surprise trophy: His victory was also his surrender to love. He was bewitched by Kelly, his whole being focused on his need for her, his every sense acutely tuned to her moods. He wanted to please her, excite her, carry her to heights neither of them had ever reached. "My Kelly-love, how I've missed you," he said, then groaned.

Suddenly she tore her hand away, hearing the joy of conquest in his voice and hating herself for succumbing to him so easily. Was she ever going to learn? Would he always be able to bypass her logic, her sense? Was she doomed to spend her life surrendering to him each time he felt like testing his romantic prowess on such an easy mark? "Dinner's out, Brannan," she said, scrambling out of her chair by jumping over the side. She ran to the picture window that overlooked the beach and stood there hugging herself again, her shoulders scrunched up as if against the cold. "I agreed to honor Kernaghan's request," she muttered, "but I don't have to celebrate the fact."

Jed straightened up and walked over to her. He'd anticipated her stubborn resistance, though he couldn't help being disappointed. He was still reeling from the joy of the previous moments, and it wasn't easy to go back to his original plan. But he gathered his self-discipline and kept his voice light as he spoke. "I agree," he told her, standing right behind her and putting his hands on her shoulders. "Dinner's not a good idea."

She stiffened but didn't try to escape his hold—not yet, not until she figured out why he'd conceded. He was up to something. "I'm glad we understand each other," she said.

Jed brushed his lips over the nape of her neck, at the same time spanning her tiny waist with his hands. He thought he'd explode from the response of his body to her warm, silky skin, and he had to exert every ounce of control at his command when he glanced down to see the slope of her breasts in the deep vee of her blouse.

Stay in control, he commanded himself. *Be aggressive, but don't act like a sailor on shore leave.* "Dinner's a dumb idea," he said into her ear, "when we can just stay here and be alone."

Kelly couldn't remain still any longer. She twisted away from Jed and raced behind the couch. "Has it occurred to you that I might have other plans, Brannan?"

"I'm sure you did," he replied pleasantly. "You don't live in a vacuum."

Kelly didn't like the way he kept agreeing with her. It was confusing. "No, I don't" she said, wary of him. "Live in a vacuum. I mean. I do have other plans."

He moved toward her. "Of course, a minute ago your other plans didn't matter, so I won't worry about them."

"A minute ago I was—" Kelly firmly closed her mouth before she made a confession. With a backward step away from Jed's slowly advancing, intimidating form, she thrust out her chin angrily. "Don't you tell me whether you'll worry about my plans or not!"

"I wouldn't dream of it, sweetheart." His advance was deliberately steady but unrushed. "I shouldn't have said what I did. I should have said your plans seemed flexible in the face of a new option."

Kelly edged backward in the direction of the front door. If she could lure him there she might be able to push him outside. "Well, they're not flexible," she answered. "I'm not going out to dinner with you."

Jed shrugged and looked surprised. "I thought we'd agreed that we wouldn't go out." He smiled. "You've given me a taste of the banquet I can have by staying right here. Why would I insist on going out?"

"I'm not a banquet!" Kelly shouted, panicking as she realized she'd backed herself into a corner in more ways than one. "I'm not even a . . . a snack! Not for you, anyway."

Jed put his hands on either side of her so she was

trapped against the wall. He leaned down and caught her pouting lower lip between his teeth and nibbled gently. "That's the appetizer," he murmured, then before she could utter a protest, covered her mouth with his and dipped his tongue inside. "That was the wine," he said when he'd tasted generously of her special sweetness. His gaze roved over her with lazy, confident possessiveness. "I can hardly wait for the main course."

"I'm hungry!" Kelly cried. Dinner in a public place was better than his private, excruciatingly effective seduction.

Jed deliberately misunderstood. "I know you're hungry, sweetheart," He trailed his finger over her delicate jawline. "We're both hungry. We have been for a long, long time."

"For food, I mean. Dinner. I'd like to take you up on your offer after all." She hated giving in, but saw no other option. "Just let me go change."

Jed studied her as if considering whether she could be trusted alone while she got dressed. "I don't think so," he said at last. "We won't find what we want in a restaurant."

He was right, Kelly thought unhappily, but she had to battle the increasing heaviness of her limbs, the heat building inside her. "I've thought about what you said . . . about the celebration for honoring Kernaghan's request. It would be terrible not to do it. With dinner," she added hastily.

Game, set, match, Jed thought, pleased with himself. "All right," he said, sighing. "If you insist. Dinner it is."

Kelly's eyes narrowed. The man had turned things around so neatly she'd been powerless to do anything but exactly what he'd wanted all along. "So I can go change my clothes?" she asked guardedly. "In private?"

Jed sighed again. "I suppose so, though it's a crime."

His gaze roved lazily over her again. "A real crime. You look great just as you are, but I know you'd like to dress up in something Kernaghan would've liked." Jed wasn't being sentimental with his suggestion. Kernaghan had been an old devil where women were concerned. If he liked a particular dress on a female, it was because it was sensual and alluring.

Kelly remembered the dress she'd bought the previous summer for a gallery opening. Kernaghan had been at the opening, and when he'd spied her his eyes had gleamed so wickedly she'd blushed. "Girl," he'd whispered privately, "you make my mustache twitch."

A gossamer creation in the blue-green color of an Aegean grotto, the dress fell in graceful folds from an off-the-shoulder neckline, then nipped in at the waist and swirled over her hips and legs with her every movement. "I won't take long getting ready," she promised, beginning to feel excited about going out with Jed. "If you don't mind waiting, I'd like to take a quick shower."

"I don't mind at all," he agreed magnanimously. He bit his tongue rather than make a comment about helping her with her shower, but the image of Kelly in the shower gave him such discomfort, he had to move away from her. *Kelly*, he thought with a deep, familiar ache. Water cascading over her smooth skin, soap gliding over her curves. . . . He cleared his throat. "I noticed a bookshelf in your living room," he said in a strained voice. "And some interesting looking volumes. I'll read while you're getting ready."

Kelly wondered when he'd had the opportunity to notice anything, but that was Jed. His powers of observation had always struck her as awesome. "I won't be long," she said again.

"I hope not, but don't rush." Now that he'd won the first battle in his long-term campaign, he could afford to play the gallant courtier. "We have all evening," he added with a smile. "The night's still very young."

So was she, Kelly thought as she went into her bedroom. She was too young to die, which was what she'd do if she let Jed destroy her again, and too young to outmaneuver a man with his experience and Irish charm. She was doomed—a lamb to the slaughter.

What *really* bothered her was that she felt a treacherous sense of elation; she was actually looking forward to the evening. She was excited, strangely happy.

It was only for tonight, she told herself. Tomorrow sanity would return, probably for Jed as well as for her.

But tonight . . .

Five

Kelly sat quietly gazing out at Traverse Bay from her vantage point next to the restaurant's wall of windows. She sipped champagne and listened as Jed gave their dinner order to the waiter in French, his accent very Gallic sounding and remarkably unself-conscious. Out of the waters of the bay a cluster of sailboats danced among ribbons of pink and gold that streamed over the surface from the sinking sun, a backdrop so effective it was as if he'd carefully contrived the setting for romance.

The dreamlike sensation Jed Brannan's presence triggered had settled around Kelly, and she almost was relaxed with him, allowing events—and Jed—to lead her where they would.

Yet on a deeper level she was tense and growing increasingly aware of how much Jed had changed. The bit of small talk they'd indulged in so far had revealed some of the man she'd loved once, but he was different too. "When did you learn French?" she asked when the waiter left.

"I took a course a couple of years ago," Jed explained. "The company's so multinational in scope now, I thought

I should pick up at least one foreign language. I lived with a French family in Provence, for a little while, and that helped a lot."

"A man of unexpected talents," Kelly murmured, wondering what other experiences he'd had, how far beyond her he'd grown. But she wanted to keep things light, so she flashed him a teasing grin. "I can't get over your brilliant fortune-telling, Brannan." Her glance swept the elegant surroundings and returned to fasten on Jed with exaggerated, wide-eyed naïveté. "You described every detail exactly, right down to the champagne and candlelight and romantic background music. Why, even the headwaiter must have tuned in to your psychic vision. He actually seemed to have expected us, and to know you on sight . . . not to mention your 'usual table.' "

Jed squirmed uneasily, wishing he'd thought to tell Jacques not to recognize him. On the other hand, he thought, it might not hurt to leave Kelly with the impression he was always bringing women to this restaurant. "No big deal," he answered. "Second sight . . . fortune-telling . . . it's a gift. Goes with being Irish."

"But I'm Irish, and I don't have the gift," Kelly argued, enjoying Jed's discomfort. "You must have learned the secrets somewhere, Brannan. Another course, perhaps? You lived with a band of gypsies at some point?"

Jed had to chuckle; how could he forget what a brat Kelly Flynn was? "You know about my gypsy period," he replied with feigned distress. "I thought it was a dark secret."

"Not to me, Brannan. I've always known you were a gypsy. Born to wander." As soon as the words were uttered Kelly wanted to call them back. They touched on serious issues and laid bare her lingering bitterness. So much, she thought disgustedly, for casual banter. Her conviction grew that she had no business playing in Jed Brannan's league.

He took full advantage of her impulsive remark. Reaching across the table to touch her wrist with a feathery caress, he spoke quietly. "My wandering days are over, Kelly. Please believe me."

Kelly's pulse raced in response, and her whole body melted under his touch. Perhaps he did have some kind of psychic gift, she thought as her gaze was caught and held by his. He seemed able to cast spells over her, blinding her to simple common sense, but succumbing completely to Jed's potent magic was the very trap she was determined to avoid. She needed an antidote, an incantation that would snap her out of her trance. Though she was prepared to give herself up to whatever pleasures the evening might offer, she utterly refused to fall in love with Jed Brannan again. "No more wandering?" she said, forcing her tongue to form another jibe or two. It was her only defense. "Actually," she went on, gaining strength with each word, "I believe you, Brannan. Let's face it. You've done your time in the field. It must be a relief to come back to a safe desk job." She managed a too-sweet smile. "Especially at your age."

Jed suppressed his grin. She was a fighter. But so was he, and he'd seen too much evidence of his power over her physical responses to be discouraged by her stubborn sauciness. "You're right," he conceded with mock sincerity. "At thirty-two I guess it's time to hang up my Indiana Jones hat and get myself fitted for a pin-striped suit."

Kelly couldn't go along with him. "You?" she said with a short laugh. "Not a chance. An occasional tie is one thing, but a pin-striped three-piecer? That'll be the day. You'd run away to the circus before you'd become an executive clone." No matter how hard she tried, she couldn't edit the admiration from her tone.

Jed sighed. "And there, in a nutshell," he said as he pretended to gaze moodily out over the bay, "is man's choice in life: to be a clown or a clone."

Kelly groaned. "Oh, please, not one of your awful puns."

He turned to look at her. "I thought I was being pretty profound."

Kelly nodded. "For you, I guess maybe it was profound. But don't quit your day job to become a philosopher, Brannan."

"I won't quit my day job for anything, now that it *is* a day job. I'm being perfectly sincere, Kelly. Any traveling I do from now on will be the kind a normal businessman does, and of course I'll travel for pleasure . . . when I show you all the wonders of the world, for instance."

Kelly couldn't help thinking he was capable of showing her the greatest wonders of the world without leaving Traverse City. "Impossible," she stated aloud. "Your limited travel, I mean. You'll never stay behind a desk. You like danger too much—excitement, exotic places with strange sounding names."

"Faraway places," Jed corrected her automatically, wondering where she'd gotten her heroic image of him. Kernaghan had embellished stories, but how far had he gone in recounting the adventures of his grandson?

"That's what I said," Kelly replied. "Faraway places with strange sounding names."

"No. You said exotic places with strange sounding names. Garbling the words again. Exotic doesn't fit the music of the song."

"So what? Clichés aren't carved in stone, you know. They're in the public domain, to be quoted or garbled at will. And I happen to like exotic better."

Jed leaned forward, instantly ready to take advantage of the opening she'd given him. "So do I, as a matter of fact. I love exotic. That's why you knock me out, Kelly Flynn."

She made a tiny but unladylike snort. "Oh, right. I'm so exotic. Sure." She leaned toward him and spoke quietly, confidentially. "This may come as a surprise to you, Brannan, but five-foot-two females with brown hair and less-than-voluptuous figures are generally not considered exotic. Not unless they're geniuses with eyeliner and know how to belly dance, neither of which are among my skills."

He picked up her champagne glass and held it to her lips. She was so surprised by his move, she cooperated by taking a sip. "Exotic," Jed told her, pleased he'd flustered her with the intimacy of the gesture, "is obviously in the eye of the connoisseur."

"Which you are, I suppose," Kelly said. She sat back in her chair and stared at her glass as Jed put it down. She'd been right from the start: He was way out of her league.

"I like to think so," he said pleasantly. "And it's true that petite females with perfect curves and rich chestnut hair are very much in demand in some circles. Especially if they know how to choose enticing dresses that ripple over their pretty bodies like ocean currents swirling around a sea nymph. Especially if they don't need eyeliner because their eyes are naturally so dramatic no mere cosmetic could enhance them."

Kelly stared at him, wondering if he really saw her that way. "You're such a cornball," she protested from sheer habit, but knew her voice revealed more fondness than mockery.

"I'll always be corny when I'm with you," he admitted. "I won't even apologize for it."

"You should," Kelly said in a small voice. The spirit

had gone out of her jibes, but she clung to them to the last second.

"Let's make a pact," Jed suggested. "I'll forgive your garbled clichés, if you'll forgive my corniness. That way we'll live happily ever after."

She opened her mouth to make a snappy comeback, but no words came out, only a long, shaky sigh. He'd done it to her again, she thought helplessly. He'd cast another spell, one charged with desire. No incantation or antidote would snap her out of this. She didn't even care about the warm pink flush that spread over her breasts and throat, a clear, erotic signal Jed wouldn't miss.

He watched Kelly's responses and suddenly felt a rush of raw male power surging through him. With a look, a touch, a word, he could sweep away all her resistance. Her total vulnerability buoyed his confidence, yet inspired a strange, protective instinct in him. He renewed his private promise never, ever to hurt Kelly again. And while he was at it, he vowed to shield her from pain and fear and loneliness to whatever extent he could. At that moment, abduction seemed like a reasonable plan. He'd simply take Kelly in his arms and spirit her away to some private spot, where he could explore the source of the rosy hue creeping over her pale skin, where he could test the outer limits of his erotic power over her—and hers over him—where he could shut out the world that had taken so much from her.

The waiter brought the shrimp cocktail, and Kelly turned to give her full attention to the sailboats that had begun returning to shore, racing against the sunset and the darkness it would bring.

"Kelly," Jed said softly.

She looked at him, blinking as if she'd been half asleep.

Jed speared a shrimp, swirled it in the spicy cocktail sauce and raised it to her lips.

"I have my own," she said, though she accepted the offering.

"But it's so much more fun to feed each other, don't you think?"

Kelly picked up her seafood fork and stabbed one of the shrimp in front of her, dipped it in the sauce, and gave it to Jed. "Now we're even," she said firmly, determined not to get too carried away by Jed's seductive little tricks. "And now let's stay on our own sides of the table, shall we? You can play mutual feeding games with the other women you squire to this restaurant."

"Your eyes aren't getting greener, are they?"

"Of course not. I don't like being one of a crowd, that's all."

"There's no crowd, Kelly."

"Tell that to the headwaiter."

Jed grinned. "Just because he recognized me, you assume I'm always here with other women?"

"A logical assumption, I'd say. It's a romantic little rendezvous spot, isn't it? Not exactly a place where sportsmen gather or where a man dines alone."

"It's perfect for entertaining clients, though."

"Sure, female clients." Kelly shot back, then popped another shrimp into her mouth.

"You *are* jealous." Jed couldn't keep the triumph out of his voice. He didn't want Kelly thinking he was a hopeless womanizer, however, so he downplayed the number of dates he'd had since he'd come back to town. They'd been nothing more than ways to pass the time anyway, though he hated being so cold-blooded about the nice young ladies he'd met at the tennis club. He'd have taken Godzilla out for dinner to occupy his mind while he got used to the emptiness of Kernaghan's house. The fact that Godzilla hadn't been around, while several lithe beauties had presented themselves as willing companions was hardly his fault. "You shouldn't be jealous," he chided Kelly. "In the first place, those other girls only made me want you all the more." It was the simple truth, but Jed couldn't blame Kelly for rolling her eyes. "And there were only a couple of them."

"A couple? That's not what I heard." Kelly swore under her breath. Why did she keep blurting things out? He didn't need to have his ego inflated by hearing her admit she'd been the slightest bit interested in his affairs.

"Okay," Jed conceded. "A few. But those women didn't mean anything to me!" That didn't sound right. He wasn't being callous, was he? "What I'm saying is, it wasn't what you think. Just because I invite a young lady out for dinner doesn't mean I—" He stopped, realizing he'd been so defensive he'd missed something Kelly had said. "What did you hear, Kelly? Who talked to you about me?"

Damn, she thought. She couldn't get anything past him. "Hair-dryer talk," she muttered.

"Hair-dryer talk?"

"At the beauty salon. The place was buzzing with gossip about your activities when you first got back. New gossip is at a premium in a small town, don't forget. Nobody talked to me, but I couldn't help overhearing." Kelly looked down at the one shrimp left in the crystal bowl. She was about to attack it with her fork when Jed reached out with one hand to catch her wrist, then with the other to pick up the shrimp, coat it with sauce, and raise it to her mouth. "I thought we'd agreed to stay on our own sides of the table," she said, refusing to accept the morsel from him.

"You agreed. I didn't." With a slow smile he stroked the sauce-covered shrimp over her lips until her tongue instinctively darted out to lick off the sauce.

The excitement that stirred deep within Kelly was almost unbearable; it was matched only by a resurgence of her fears. Jed was far too experienced for her. She was going to make a fool of herself tonight, and by morning he wouldn't have the slightest interest in her. By then he'd have realized, if he hadn't already, that stirring up nostalgic feelings for lost loves and simpler times couldn't form the basis of a relationship. She snapped the shellfish from him, almost taking his fingers with it.

"Sweetheart," Jed scolded, his eyes twinkling with delight, "I know you hunger for me, but try to control your appetite until we're in a more private setting, won't you?"

Kelly considered driving a seafood fork through his heart, but suddenly saw how silly she was being. She laughed. "Okay, Brannan," she conceded. "I'll do my best to keep a lid on the raging fires of passion inside me, but you'll have to cooperate and let me feed myself. Deal?" Though she spoke lightly, she meant every word.

"Deal?" he repeated. "I'm not sure. I enjoy watching your raging fires burst into uncontrollable flames. Then again, I have my own conflagration to control. All I can promise is that I'll make a sincere effort to behave."

"Maybe we should call in the fire department," Kelly suggested.

"It wouldn't do any good." Jed paused while the busboy cleared their plates and the waiter brought the main course. "You see, it's spontaneous combustion," he continued as soon as they were alone again. "The boys at the fire department don't know how to handle it. Nobody does. That's why even I can't guarantee anything. But I'll tell you this, Kelly: If you find yourself suddenly being ravished under the grand piano, don't blame me."

"Why?" she asked. "Won't you be the ravisher?"

"Definitely, but it won't be my fault. You'll have to look closer to home for the person responsible. Take your dress, for instance—the way it bares your shoulders; the way the elastic neckline and the waist look so easy to push down; the way the tips of your breasts get all swollen against the thin material. It happens every time those fires inside you burn a little hotter. It happens a lot, Kelly."

It was happening that very moment, she realized.

"Another thing," he added in a low, raspy voice. "Your legs are bare. Even though the skirt of your dress reaches to midcalf, your sandals give away the fact that you're not wearing stockings. It makes me wonder just how little you are wearing under that dress, which in turn makes me wonder how you could expect to play with fire and not get burned."

Kelly stared down at her plate. It was true, every word. When she'd worn the dress to the gallery opening she'd also worn panty hose and a strapless bra. The dropped, bare-shoulder neckline hadn't been quite as dropped as it was tonight, and there had been no irresistible stimulation to make her nipples rise and harden until they almost poked through the cloth. She cleared her throat. "With all this talk of fire and heat," she managed to say, "our dinner's getting cold."

The hell with dinner, Jed thought, but he nodded. "You're right. It looks good too."

Kelly tasted the moist trout encrusted with almonds. "It's perfect," she murmured. "What I'd like to know, though, is why you had to order in French. The trout is from the Great Lakes, and the French don't have a monopoly on almonds, so why the *truite almondine* or whatever it was you said?"

Jed shrugged. "The French have managed to create the mystique that all things related to sensual pleasure are their special domain. I'm not sure they're wrong.

Thus, the French menu in a restaurant on the shores of Lake Michigan."

"How long did you live in France?" she asked, glad to steer the conversation to a less provocative topic.

"I lived with a family in Provence for three months, and then I spent a few weeks in Paris to check out a company for possible acquisition. I've kicked around the country for an odd week here and there, sometimes vacationing and sometimes doing business."

Kelly's insecurities returned. Jed had 'kicked around' France; he'd lived in Provence, and Paris, probably testing the French mystique of sensual superiority. She was so ill-prepared for the person he'd become, so pitifully inexperienced in every way. Geographically she'd never been anywhere more cosmopolitan than Chicago. Sensually, she'd never been anywhere at all, except for the uncompleted journeys into bliss Jed himself had taken her on. "Traverse City must seem dull after the places you've been," she remarked.

"Not in the least. Traverse City holds a lot of precious memories for me—all those summers away from the humidity of New York, all the friends here who welcomed me back like a prodigal son just because they liked Kernaghan so much . . ."

"I think some of those friends like you for yourself," Kelly put in. Was it possible he had his own insecurities? She discarded the idea as wishful thinking. Simply because she felt vulnerable, she wanted everyone else to have the same problem—especially Jed.

He was quiet for a moment, mulling over Kelly's assertion. Was she right? Did some people accept him on his own terms? He'd grown so used to the empty flattery of favor seekers and corporate sycophants, he wasn't sure he could spot real friendship. He was cynical about women perhaps because his attractiveness to them was always intensified if they learned he was heir to Kernaghan Explorations.

Except Kelly. She didn't care a fig who he was, how wealthy he was, or what he could offer her. To Kelly, he'd always been and would always be just Jed.

He grinned inwardly. Nowadays he was just "Brannan." He hoped he'd change that—later tonight, if he had his way.

They finished their main course, shared a slice of almond-liqueur cheesecake for dessert, then sat chatting over coffee and cognac, catching up on the past. Kelly discovered how deeply fascinated Jed was by Celtic lore. He'd studied the subject more fully than she had, in fact, and for a while she forgot her nervousness as they participated in a lively exchange of ancient tales.

Eventually they couldn't pretend to want more coffee or cognac. The moment arrived when they had to leave the safety of the public restaurant and face each other in private. It was a moment each had secretly dreaded yet eagerly anticipated.

They were quiet in the car on the way back to Kelly's place. Jed sensed a renewed closeness with her, and though he wanted to make love to her to seal that closeness, he didn't want his impatience to scare her off. Kelly remained silent as her insecurities resurfaced. What if Jed wanted to make love to her? she asked herself. She died inside at the thought of disappointing him.

At her door she dug out her key and tried to fit it into the lock, but her hand shook so badly Jed had to take over the task. He pushed the door open and held it while Kelly went into the house; then he followed her. Inside he hesitated, waiting for her to flip on the lights and perhaps give him some signal whether she wanted him to stay or to go.

But her signals were mixed as she turned to look up

at him. Her eyes were dark, her expression soft with invitation, yet her body was stiff with tension. "Thanks for dinner," she murmured.

Jed took her words as a dismissal. He smiled, deciding he'd made enough progress for the moment. *Patience*, he told himself. "Thank *you* for dinner, Kelly," he said, leaning down to give her a chaste little peck on her cheek. "It was my pleasure."

Kelly watched him go out the door and walk toward his car. It was happening all over again, she thought. After arousing her desire, he was leaving. Perhaps he'd begun to sense her inexperience. Or perhaps he was just being a gentleman. She didn't want him to be a gentleman. She wanted him to make love to her. "Wait," she cried as he reached his car.

He turned, a clear question in his eyes.

"Wait," Kelly said again, then was suddenly shocked into silence by her own actions. What was she supposed to do? Come right out and say it? She took a deep breath and opened her mouth to do just that. *No more shyness, no more holding back*, she vowed. She was long overdue for collecting on Jed Brannan's sensual promises. She'd go ahead and blurt it out: Make love to me. Tonight. Now. "I . . ." She cleared her throat and tried again, only to hear herself say, "I'm going to have a cup of tea. Would you like some?"

Six

Tea, Jed repeated silently. It wasn't the response he'd hoped for, but who was he to nitpick? "I'd love some tea," he said with real enthusiasm.

Kelly wanted to hug him for being such a good sport. They were both still full from the coffee and cognac, yet he was graciously accepting her dumb offer of tea.

She stepped back inside the house, and Jed followed her. "I meant to tell you that I like what you've done with this place," he remarked as she closed the door. His glance took in the refinished antiques, the bright slipcovers and curtains, the hooked scatter rugs that warmed the gleaming hardwood floor. He remembered in detail all Kernaghan's reports of Kelly's progress in transforming a run-down cottage into a cozy home. "I like it a lot."

"It's comfortable," Kelly said, absently engaging the new dead-bolt lock on her door.

"Comfy-cozy," Jed amended. His regret was instantaneous. "I'm sorry, Kelly. I forgot where I'd picked up that phrase. I wish I weren't so thoughtless at times.

You'd think I, of all people, would realize how little unexpected reminders can hurt."

Kelly knew his distress was genuine. For the first time since their separation, she admitted to herself how deeply Jed hated to inflict pain of any kind. "Don't worry," she reassured him. "The fact is, I appreciate your saying that. I like to think Mom would have pronounced my house comfy-cozy. It was the highest praise she could give, so you couldn't have chosen a better compliment."

Jed took Kelly's hand in his, relieved by her calm response and glad they finally could talk about the past. "Your mother was never impressed by trendy styles," he recalled aloud. "Maureen was too down-to-earth for that sort of thing."

"Too sentimental, you mean," Kelly added, surprised by the ease with which she was able to carry on the conversation. For a long time the mere mention of her parents had set her off on a crying spree.

She tugged on Jed's hand to lead him into the living room. "Mom was into the accumulated-treasure school of interior design," she went on. "She believed in rescuing old pieces of furniture, not to save money, but to preserve the memories that were imprinted on them." Kelly smiled, a little embarrassed. "Like I said, she was sentimental."

"Judging by the work you've done here," Jed said quietly, "you're from the same school as your mom."

"How do you know it's my work?" Kelly asked. Most people assumed she'd hired someone to handle the details involved.

Jed didn't object to revealing his source. "Kernaghan used to drop in on you quite often, didn't he?"

Kelly nodded, frowning. She'd looked forward to those visits, both for the lively chats and the news of Jed. It hadn't occurred to her that Kernaghan was acting as a double agent.

Jed saw her troubled expression, and he hastened to explain. "My grandfather was a great letter writer. He used to describe the comings and goings of this town so vividly, I felt as if I were right here all the time." Drawing Kelly to the large window facing the beach, Jed put his arm around her shoulders. "Look at that lake," he murmured. "I used to read those letters over and over. I'd get as homesick as a kid suffering through the first year of summer camp, but I'd keep reading. Kernaghan would take me on his strolls through town, pausing for a chat here, stopping in for pipe tobacco there, having a whiskey with some old crony . . ." Jed hesitated, feeling a lump in his throat. He held Kelly a little closer and went on. "The old man would also drop in to see how Kelly was getting along with her new cottage."

Kelly rested her head against Jed's shoulder, her tension gradually slipping away. "I used to plan my days around those visits," she said with a fond smile. "I always took a break when Kernaghan arrived and had a whole new fund of energy to draw on by the time he'd left."

"And you needed it," Jed added affectionately. "Kernaghan told me how you tackled decorating this place and about the flea-market furniture you'd picked up. What happened to the things from your parents' house, anyway?"

"I kept a few pieces, but the rest is in storage. For how long, I don't know. I didn't have the heart to sell anything, because it would have seemed like a betrayal, but most of my parents' furniture was just too big for my cottage."

"Maybe once your brother gets a place of his own," Jed suggested.

"Mike's not the sentimentalist Mom and I are . . . were . . ." She laughed softly. "He's definitely into trendy furniture styles. So I have no idea why I'm keeping all that stuff. I simply can't make myself get rid of it."

"In some ways, Kelly Flynn, you're living in the wrong era. You don't quite fit into this disposable society of ours. Permanence and continuity . . . those are your values."

Kelly slid her arm around Jed's waist, remembering how safe she'd felt with him. Not just physically safe, but emotionally safe. He understood her and respected the things that mattered to her. "The trouble is," she reminded both of them, "permanence is an illusion."

Jed wasn't surprised by her statement. So much of what had been important to Kelly had simply disappeared. "But there's continuity," he said gently. "I guess that's what we represent."

Neither of them spoke for a while. The only sounds were the shallow waves lapping the nearby shore and the birch leaves rustling in the evening breeze.

"So Kernaghan told you all about my cottage," Kelly said, breaking the silence. She was surprised that she'd been the subject of regular reports.

"And about the way you scrubbed and polished and stripped paint and applied paint and sewed slipcovers all day and half the night." Jed hesitated, then repeated his grandfather's expression. "Trying to drown out the wails of the banshees. That's what Kernaghan said you were doing."

Kelly closed her eyes and swallowed hard, then spoke in a soft voice. "He was right. Sometimes I regretted buying this cottage, when the wind would come howling over the water and shake the windows as if it were trying to get in at me. Work was my therapy."

"It silenced the banshees?" Jed asked gently.

Kelly nodded. "And then I wished it hadn't," she said

so softly Jed had to strain to hear. "Because there was no warning about Kernaghan, and I kept thinking if I hadn't been such a coward, if I'd known, maybe I could have . . ." She stopped trying to talk; it was too difficult.

Jed wrapped his arms around her, holding her tight, as much to comfort himself as to comfort her. "You do know that's only the old superstitious foolishness we grew up with, don't you?"

"I know," Kelly said, resting her cheek on his hard chest. It amazed her that Jed's body could be so un-yielding, so strong, so capable of dealing with any kind of work or physical endurance, while his spirit was so gentle. "But knowing in my head and knowing in my soul are two different things."

Jed's arms tightened around her. "You shouldn't have gone through all that alone," he said fiercely. "Not the work, not the grief, not the lonely nights of being scared."

"For most of it I wasn't totally alone," Kelly protested, feeling guilty for accepting Jed's sympathy when his own grief was sharp and fresh. "Kernaghan was the best friend anyone could have had."

"It should have been me," Jed said. "You were right, you know. I realized it too late, but I should have found a way for us to stay together."

Kelly had recently done some honest thinking of her own on that score. "Maybe I could've made it a less black-and-white choice," she suggested. "I do under-stand now why you told me to date others, but then I took it as a straight rejection. You were a summer person, and I was an unsophisticated local, and sum-mer was over."

Jed released her enough so he could cradle her face in his hands, stroking her lips with his thumbs. "You don't think that way now, do you?" he asked, marvel-ing at the way Kelly's eyes reflected the starlight.

She hesitated. "I'm not sure what I think," she answered truthfully. "Except that I don't want to think. Not tonight." She placed her hands over his and closed her eyes. "May I tell you something else I don't want tonight?"

"Of course," Jed replied, bracing himself and deciding he'd be understanding no matter what she said. "What don't you want, Kelly?"

She opened her eyes and grinned mischievously. "I don't want any tea."

It took a minute for Jed to catch on. He cocked his head to one side, a bemused smile on his face. Then the truth dawned, and pure joy welled up inside him. He pulled Kelly hard against his body and buried his face in the chestnut silk of her hair. "Before we . . ." He chuckled hoarsely. "Before we don't have tea," he murmured, using Kelly's odd but original euphemism for lovemaking, "I have to tell you something. I'm home to stay, and the only thing that matters to me is right here in my arms. I'm not just one of the summer people. And for the record, Kelly, I'm not a womanizer and never have been. Those girls at the—"

"That's four somethings," Kelly interrupted, drawing back and placing her index finger over Jed's lips. "And I didn't want to think tonight, remember?"

He smiled, once again reining in his impatience. He'd wanted to get everything out into the open, everything settled, commitments made. Full-speed-ahead Brannan, his colleagues in the company had called him more than once—with justification. Well, he was going to have to cut back on the throttle. Tonight, Kelly wanted only to make love. It wasn't such a bad compromise, but he had to hear her say it. That commitment he had to have. "What *do* you want, sweetheart?" he asked innocently.

Kelly hesitated. *Teach me*, she wanted to tell him.

Be patient with me. Please, please don't expect too much of me.

But she didn't have the confidence to be that honest. Twining her arms around Jed's neck she stood on tiptoe and touched her lips to the corner of his mouth. "Surprise me," she whispered.

Jed turned his head enough to capture her teasing lips with his own. He nibbled gently as deep, carefree laughter rose from within him. "Brat," he said with affection. "Even at a time like this you're a brat." In one quick move, he scooped her up in his arms.

Kelly gasped, delighted. She didn't have to think or make decisions or even pretend to know what she was doing. Jed was carrying her to the bedroom exactly as she'd always wanted him to, and he'd make love to her, and she simply would follow his lead. With her arms wound around his neck, she nuzzled his throat, trailing her lips over his warm, scented skin, breathing in his fragrance of spice and citrus and musk. Her tongue darted out for a taste, and instantly she was addicted. Her lips and tongue traveled over every delicious inch of his strong neck and chiseled jawline, then leisurely toyed with his earlobe.

"Maybe I like brats," Jed murmured as his body responded to her exquisite torment. He walked slowly to the bedroom, eager to reach his destination but enjoying the journey too much to rush it.

Kelly's soft breasts, crushed against Jed's chest, absorbed the syncopated pounding of his heartbeat. She could feel the uneven rise and fall of his breathing, and she knew she needn't blame the fact that he was carrying her; she was like a weightless doll in his arms. An unfamiliar sensation of power surged through her. She'd known all along what Jed could do to her, but suddenly she realized what she could do to him. The knowledge opened up whole new vistas for her. Her mouth sought and found an inviting hollow above the edge of his collar; she exulted in his small, sudden intakes of breath when her tongue touched a pulse spot.

Her eyelashes fluttered open long enough for Kelly to see that Jed was about to lower her to the bed. He set her down as carefully and gently as if she were a piece of fragile crystal; his smile made her feel infinitely more precious.

He sat on the edge of the mattress and placed his hands on either side of her. "By the way," he said in a seductive voice. "What's my name, sweetheart?"

The question puzzled Kelly for a moment. Then she laughed huskily. She would call him Jed tonight; there was no doubt about that, but she didn't want to cheat him of a battle.

"I'm waiting," he prompted, undoing his tie.

Kelly pretended to think very hard, then at last said, "Rumpelstiltskin?"

Jed's eyes glimmered with laughter as he watched the impish quirk of Kelly's mouth. "Rumpelstiltskin," he repeated thoughtfully, as if giving the name serious consideration. Finally he shrugged, "What the hell, I can live with it." Suddenly he bent down to capture Kelly's lower lip between his teeth, nipping the soft, moist flesh until it was swollen and pink and Kelly's breathing was as ragged as his own, her heart thumping to the same wild rhythm, her back arching instinctively. "And you," he murmured, brushing his lips across her cheekbones, "are the beautiful young maiden at her spinning wheel, but instead of spinning straw into gold, you're spinning invisible cords to bind me as your prisoner." He raised his head and looked down at her. "Or am I being corny again?"

Kelly sighed deeply. "Oh, do be corny, please. Just as corny as you like."

"So you won't mind if I tell you," Jed whispered,

lightly trailing his fingers over her face and throat, teasing at the edge of her neckline, "that you're the very fairest maiden in this or any land?"

"To quote a certain . . ." A shiver of excitement passed through Kelly's body as Jed made feathery little strokes over the slope of her breasts. She tried to speak again. "To quote a certain . . . *eloquent* . . . Irishman," she managed to say, "I can live with it."

"Oh, you will, sweetheart," Jed told her, determined to leave no question between them about his intentions. "You'll live with it for the rest of your days." To seal the vow he gently tugged down the bodice of her dress, then dipped his head to touch his lips to each creamy mound, each rose-hued tip. "I love your breasts," he told her, and made her believe his words by relishing their sweet softness. "I've always loved them."

Kelly heard Jed's words, but only vaguely. She sensed that he was warning her against taking this step in their relationship lightly, against playing at love, but she set such thoughts aside. She'd told him she didn't want to think. Tonight was for feeling, and what he was making her feel destroyed her thinking processes anyway. The touch of his lips and tongue to her swelling nipples lit a fuse that burned within seconds to the very core of her, setting off a fiery explosion.

"You're so beautiful, Kelly," Jed told her, sweeping her dress off her in one bold, deft motion.

"And very wicked," Kelly murmured. "You see, you were right about how little I wore under my dress."

He smiled and began caressing her with gentle fingertips, taking time to learn all the contours of her body. "Amazing," he said quietly as he continued his exploration. "We still have so much in common, sweetheart. It just so happens I like wicked. *Very* wicked's even better. As long as you're only wicked with me, feel free to take it as far as you wish."

Another statement of intention, Kelly thought, but she closed her eyes and floated in relaxed, sensual bliss.

Jed's hands brushed across the wisp of lace Kelly still wore, a flimsy bit of cloth that was more tantalizing than protective. He tested his control to the limit, outlining with his finger the design of the lace, tracing the bikini's high-cut curve over her thighs.

"You're driving me wild," Kelly cried softly.

"And myself," Jed admitted. He bent to trail his tongue over the path his hands had just blazed. "But that's the idea, isn't it?" he added, his lips hot against the cool satin of her thigh.

"I'm not sure I'll survive," Kelly protested, though she was prepared to endure the delicious torture.

Jed smiled, continuing to arouse her until she was so alive to his every touch he wasn't sure he'd survive himself. He was awed by Kelly's eager, guileless responses, her total compliance, her utter trust. "No wonder poor old Rumpelstiltskin flew into such a rage," he said lightly, trying to diminish some of the overwhelming need in his body. He wanted their time together to last, to be so perfect, so profoundly moving, there would be no doubt left in Kelly's mind that their love was stronger than ever. "Who could blame the guy," Jed went on, "when he realized his fair maiden had eluded him?" He pressed a kiss to the inside of Kelly's knee. "I'd probably do the same myself," he added, talking aimlessly in a losing battle against a burning, aching desire.

Kelly gave a shaky sigh. Her eyes were closed as she drifted through a whole new universe of unimagined pleasure, and when she opened them to look at Jed, her insides contracted in intense excitement at the sight of him bent over her body. "But Rumpelstiltskin wasn't Jed Brannan," she managed to say.

Jed let his caresses wander upward. "I'm gratified," he said when he reached her waist. "But tell me how old Rumpie and I are different. Why should I . . ." He paused to swirl his tongue around each of her nipples, drawing them to eager attention. "Why should I be lucky enough to have you, when he ended up alone and miserable?"

Kelly reached up to undo the buttons of Jed's shirt. Her hands were shaking so much, she kept fumbling. After she'd done all but rip two buttons off, Jed grinned, and took over the job. He slid out of his jacket, tossed it and his tie to a nearby chair, and finished undoing his shirt. "You haven't answered me," he reminded her.

Kelly couldn't remember what he'd asked her. She watched in rapt fascination as he opened his shirt and stripped it off. Her concentration was focused on the thatch of light brown curls that matted his bronzed chest. The obvious strength of his muscles took her breath away. "Oh, dear," she murmured. He'd been a beautiful male seven years ago—now he was godlike. "You asked—" She swallowed hard—"how you are different from Rumpelstiltskin." A slow smile curved her lips. "Let me count the ways."

He stood and began undoing his belt, basking in Kelly's open admiration. She gave him a new kind of confidence, made him feel desirable as a man, someone she wanted as much as he wanted her.

"Rumpelstiltskin lost," Kelly said softly, attentive to Jed's every move, "because fair maidens are not airheads. They know the difference between a Prince Charming waking them with a kiss and some ugly toad with royal pretensions making a crude pass."

Jed choked on a sudden bubble of laughter, then quickly tried to cover it by divesting himself of the rest of his clothes.

"What's so funny?" Kelly asked, her eyes wide. She'd half expected to be frightened at this point, but she wasn't frightened at all. She could hardly wait to feel his warm, masculine hardness against her softness.

Jed hadn't realized a female could look so unabashedly, innocently lecherous. "You're funny," he said affectionately, leaning down to kiss both of her inner thighs. "You managed to scramble at least three fairy tales into one confusing explanation." He moved to the foot of the bed and cupped his hand under one of her ankles, then lifted her leg and removed her sandal. "There you go, Cinderella," he murmured, pressing a kiss to her instep.

She raised herself up on her elbows, watching him. She didn't plan to miss a thing. "I hope I don't turn into a pumpkin when this is over."

Jed removed her other shoe. "You could, you know. It's a definite danger. That's why we must never stop." Still touching his lips to her instep, he moved back to the side of the bed and nibbled his way upward.

"Never?" Kelly repeated dreamily, sinking to her pillow.

"Never." He hooked his fingers under the elastic of her panties and drew them slowly down her legs, struggling to control the urgency building inside him.

Kelly was surprised by her utter abandon, her strange sense of liberation. It felt right to be naked and in bed with Jed, right and natural and beautiful. She held out her arms to him, wanting to feel the whole length of his body against hers.

"Sweetheart," Jed whispered as he went to her, wrapping himself around her and stroking her hair as he showered kisses over her face. "I love you. I've never stopped loving you. I'll always love you."

Kelly ran her palms over his back, glorying in the smooth, warm skin that was so taut over the hard ripple of muscle. She sought his mouth, meeting the thrust of his tongue with her own.

"And I love you, Jed," she admitted. "I can't pretend to either of us that I don't."

His arms tightened around her. Kelly realized that she'd said his first name, but she wasn't sorry to lose the battle. "Make love to me," she urged. "This is . . . so very long overdue. Make love to me, Jed." She smiled. "Please, Jed. Love me."

He heard her words and his senses reeled. Her surrender was total. "Be patient," he was shocked to hear himself say. Was Brannan preaching about patience? He wanted to use every ounce of his strength, experience, and willpower to carry Kelly to heights she'd never reached before. "Trust me," he said. "We have lots of time, and there's so much to make up for."

He then devoted himself to the rewarding task of pleasuring the woman he loved. His hands and lips seemed inspired by a playful yet reverent inventiveness of their own. He found himself in a trancelike state, his movements guided not by his intellect, but by a force working in and through him, permeating his being until he was merely an instrument, a physical expression of its limitless power—and that force was pure, unconditional love.

He'd asked Kelly to trust him, and she did, giving him total power over her, setting aside every vestige of her own will. He used her gift for the sole purpose of leading her to peaks of ecstasy even he hadn't dreamed existed.

The moment inevitably arrived when Jed knew he couldn't hold back any longer. He moved over Kelly and bent his head to capture her mouth, delving into its innermost recesses with deep thrusts of his tongue, imitating the way he would soon thrust into her secret warmth.

Kelly thought only dimly about the step she was about to take. She was euphoric, completely centered on the moment. Nothing existed beyond the special dimension she and Jed had entered. "Please, Jed," she whispered. "Please don't stop now."

"I won't stop," he told her, then watched her face as he slowly, gently entered her.

Kelly cried out as reality rushed in at her in a stab of pain, then receded just as quickly. She saw the puzzled concern in Jed's eyes and felt his hesitation within her. "You promised you wouldn't stop," she said in a low, urgent tone.

"My Lord, Kelly," he said hoarsely. "What—"

"Don't, please don't stop. I want you so much, Jed. If you love me . . . then *love* me!"

Jed studied her for a timeless moment, at last succumbing to her entreaties and his own terrible need. He knew what had happened, and though it confused him, he felt a renewed, all encompassing tenderness toward Kelly. He held her close, so close she was almost a part of him. Their bodies were joined, throbbing in time to a single heartbeat.

Jed didn't want it to end—ever—but his self-control was slipping away. When Kelly wrapped her legs around him and pulled him deeper into her, he had to give in to the irresistible surge that coursed through him, carrying Kelly with him into sensual oblivion.

Kelly laced her fingers through Jed's hair, stroking him with a soothing touch as if she were trying to comfort him. She loved the low, unintelligible and uncontrolled sounds he made at the very moment of their union. She'd never known a man could be vulnerable. A thin layer of her fear suddenly drifted away.

A long time later as Jed lay beside Kelly, her head nestled into his shoulder and a blanket pulled over them, he finally asked the question Kelly had hoped he wouldn't. "Why?" he said quietly.

She hedged. "Why what?"

"Why everything? For starters, why didn't you tell me?"

Kelly shrugged. Reason was beginning to overcome passion, and she herself was wondering about a lot of things.

"If you'd told me," Jed prompted, "I'd have been . . . more careful."

"I didn't want you to be careful," Kelly replied truthfully. "I wanted you to make love to me, and you did." She pressed her lips to his shoulder. "Beautifully."

"I hurt you," he muttered.

"No, you didn't. All right, for a second maybe, but it was worth it, Jed. Believe me."

He hoped she was telling him the truth, thought she probably was. Her ecstatic cries and the wild abandon of her movements left little room for doubt, but he was still puzzled. "I don't get it," he said. "I can't fathom why you wouldn't tell me."

"I was praying you wouldn't notice," Kelly said in a small voice.

He kissed the top of her head. "Kind of difficult not to notice something like that."

"You never know," she argued. "I've read a little about it. A man can't always tell. And really, Jed, suppose you were me? How would you have said it? How would you tell a person you were a . . . a twenty-five-year-old . . . *virgin!*"

Jed raised himself on one elbow and looked down at her, not sure whether to laugh, or scold her or send up a cheer. The implications of what he'd learned were just beginning to hit him. He wondered if they were dawning on Kelly too. "You're feeling humiliated about being a virgin?" he asked, checking to be sure he'd heard correctly.

"Well, wouldn't you be? I mean . . . it just isn't done!"

Kelly sat up, drawing her knees to her chest and clasping her arms around them.

Jed wasn't certain how to handle the situation. "I'm sure your . . . condition . . . wasn't due to a lack of offers," he said. He sat up and began rubbing Kelly's back. "Let's talk about it, sweetheart. How did it happen? Or not happen, I guess I should say."

Kelly glanced at him to see if he was teasing. "I guess I never got around to it until now."

"You've had some serious relationships," Jed pointed out, working on the rapidly tensing muscles in the back of Kelly's neck. "Or so I heard, anyway. You were engaged—a piece of news I wasn't likely to overlook or forget."

"I had no serious relationships," she said slowly, only now realizing the truth of her words. "I had several long-term platonic ones some people interpreted the wrong way, including, unfortunately, a couple of the relationshippees."

"Relationshippees?" Jed repeated, smiling as he kissed her shoulder. "I'd forgotten how you tend to compose words on the spot. I'm trying to get reacquainted with your peculiar way of putting things."

"This is hardly the time to make fun of me, Brannan."

"We're back to 'Brannan,' are we?" Jed slid his hands around Kelly's body to cup her breasts in his palms. He knew his most effective approach and wasn't the least bit reluctant to use it. "Never mind. I know the cure, and I think it's the perfect time to make fun of you. You're taking yourself too seriously."

"Easy for you to say," Kelly said. She knew she was overreacting to the situation, but she felt guilty about keeping her virginity from Jed. It was irresponsible— for reasons she hoped he wouldn't get around to mentioning.

He caressed her breasts with casual, almost absent-minded familiarity. "Tell you what," he told her. "I'll let you in on a troubling secret I've just discovered about myself, if it'll make you happy."

Kelly leaned back against him, closing her eyes, amazed at the deep well of desire within her that Jed could tap into whenever he chose. "A troubling secret about you? Sure, that might help."

"I don't know," he said. "You're too eager to hear this. I have to walk a fine line. You see, I've discovered I'm kind of . . ." He searched for the right word. Pleased? Satisfied? "Thrilled," he said finally. "I'm thrilled to be the first man to make love to you. That's chauvinistic of me, as I'm sure you'd be quick to point out, but it's true. I'm thrilled."

Kelly arched her back as Jed toyed with the soft buds of her nipples. "You are?" she said. "You're honestly thrilled?"

"Honestly."

She felt she had to ask him. "What if I hadn't been?"

He nibbled on her ear for a moment before answering. "No problem. I assumed you weren't. Was your fiancé some kind of eunuch?"

Kelly wasn't interested in discussing her former fiancé, but she tried to answer truthfully. "On the contrary. He was very popular with women. In retrospect I'd say he proposed marriage because he saw it as the only way to get me into bed."

"Why was it the only way to get you into bed?" Jed asked carefully, hating his curiosity but unable to quell it.

"Good question. Robert—my fiancé—often asked me the same thing. When I realized the answer was that I didn't want to and probably wouldn't even after we were married, I suggested Robert might be happier with someone else. And he is. He's married to a gorgeous creature who's always being mistaken for Kathleen Turner."

Jed breathed in very slowly and exhaled just as slowly. He didn't want Kelly to know how relieved he was. She'd never loved the guy. He wasn't a big issue between them. "So here we are," he said, shifting Kelly so she was half reclining in his arms, her green eyes gazing up at him. "I'm the first"—he grinned—"and *only* . . . lover in Kelly Flynn's life after all."

She smiled, but tried to sound severe. "You really are a chauvinist, Brannan. Wanting a virgin at your age, with your level of sophistication and enlightenment."

"No matter," he said lightly, smoothing his palm over the curve of her slender hip. "You'll soon cure me of my chauvinism. Look at this situation from my point of view. I thought events—and my own stupidity—had robbed me of a privilege that might have been mine, and it suddenly turns out I was wrong." He bent his head to give Kelly a long, meaningful kiss. "It turns out," he murmured, "you waited for me."

Kelly was shaken by the confident possessiveness of the kiss . . . and by the knowledge that Jed was right. Without being aware of it she'd waited for him all along. But what if he hadn't come back to her? Would she have spent her life waiting like some modern-day Miss Havisham? The thought startled her. She didn't want to be dependent on any man—on anyone. "Don't go letting your ego run away with you again," she said. "After Robert I concentrated on my studies. And then . . . well, the accident . . . I had neither the time nor inclination for socializing, much less romance."

"Well, welcome back," Jed said cheerfully.

Kelly couldn't help smiling. "It's good to be back," she admitted, then closed her eyes as Jed's fingers found the particular spot that he'd discovered earlier, one that instantly drove every thought from her mind but her desire for him.

Jed wrestled with his natural impatience and lost. "So how soon can we set the date?" he asked quietly.

Kelly opened her eyes and stared at him. "Set what date?"

"The wedding date. I've told you my intentions from the beginning."

She raised herself to a sitting position, gently moving his hand from her body. "And I told you mine. I don't want to get married, Jed."

He toyed with a strand of her hair. He'd expected this reaction, but he wasn't going to let her get away with it. Her actions completely belied her words. "Yes you do, Kelly. You want marriage, and you want to marry me. You want to bear our children . . ."

"Where did you get that idea?" Kelly demanded, edging away from him and regarding him warily, changing her position so she was facing him and kneeling, her hands reaching for the blanket to cover herself.

Jed pulled the blanket away from her, his gaze sweeping her body with such intensity she felt as if he were branding her. "We'll work things out, Kelly," he said in a tight, controlled voice. "From now on there'll be nothing but honesty between us. And we don't put up false barriers—like blankets to cover nakedness, like hypocrisy to cover nameless fears."

"What are you talking about?" Kelly asked.

"You tell me. If not now, later. Whenever you're ready. Whenever you find the courage to be honest about what you felt tonight."

Kelly opened her mouth to offer a few well-chosen insults, but closed it again without uttering a single word. She bowed her head and covered her face with her hands. "I'm mixed up, Jed."

He melted at her forlorn tone, and reached for her, gently gathering her close. "I know, Kelly. If I were a whole lot wiser, I'd be able to figure out what's going on in your head, but I can't. You've got me pretty mixed up too. But I'm not confused about loving you, or about whether you love me."

"Something happened to me tonight, Jed," she told him. "For a while there, nothing mattered. I didn't care about consequences or reality." She looked at him, wishing he could read her feelings in her eyes and explain them to her. "The only reality," she admitted slowly, "was you."

Jed lowered her to the bed, muffling her weak protest with a kiss. He stroked her body soothingly, then began the erotic caresses that brought her instantly alive. As he moved over her and eased into her for the second time, he spoke quietly. "The only reality," he murmured as she opened to him without reserve, "is us." Burying himself deeper and deeper into her welcoming warmth, he spoke again, willing the idea to take root and grow. "Us, Kelly. A single, indivisible entity."

The words haunted Kelly the next day as she tried to concentrate on work in her studio, idly sketching designs for the Beauregarde portrait, but her mind kept focusing on one simple truth: Marriage to anyone—especially Jed—terrified her. Yet she had knowingly, willingly, deliberately affirmed their union by risking . . . wanting . . . the chance to have his child.

Another thought nagged at her and undermined everything she tried to think of or do. Finally she had to face it: The telephone had been completely silent the whole time Jed had been with her.

Seven

Jed slammed down the receiver and cursed the telephone, blaming it for his troubles. "What's happened to the famous luck of the Irish?" he grumbled to the picture on his desk. His grandfather's face smiled back at him, a familiar twinkle of amusement in the old man's eyes, which didn't help Jed's mood any. "It's not funny," he muttered, dialing the phone again and getting another busy signal. "This is the last number I have where Kelly might be this morning, and I can't get an answer. This is just great. Now what do I—?" Jed stopped abruptly, realizing his office door had opened.

Diane Grant was staring at him as if he'd gone mad. Maybe she was right, he thought sourly, aware he'd been complaining to a photograph and beating on a telephone. "Are the arrangements made?" he asked the secretary in as pleasant a tone as he could summon.

She nodded. "All set. Sorry I interrupted you in the middle of—of a conference call."

Jed added diplomacy to Diane's list of sterling qualities. Grateful for the out she was offering, he went along with her. "No problem. I'd just finished. Have you talked to Dorothy?"

Diane nodded again. "You're all packed. She's even put in some insect repellent."

"You two are something else." Jed began stuffing vital papers into his briefcase. "If I do manage to pull this project together, it'll be because of the backup I get here, and that's no exaggeration."

"I know," Diane said airily, though she flashed a smile that told Jed she appreciated his praise. "The reason I barged in on you when you're trying to get organized is that there's someone to see you. A hunk, to be specific. Tall, dark, handsome . . . Is he married?"

Jed remembered his ten o'clock appointment. "Tony Leonard. I'd almost forgotten. Will you tell him to come right in, Diane?"

She raised a brow.

Jed frowned, then realized he hadn't answered her question. "No. He's not married, not engaged, not even going with anyone special."

A moment later Diane held open the door while Tony walked into the office. He stretched out his hand to Jed, but his gaze was locked on Diane.

"Is she available?" Tony asked after Diane had closed the door.

"And interested," Jed answered, gripping his friend's hand.

"You wouldn't mind if I asked her out?"

Jed waved Tony to a chair and went to pour two cups of coffee. "Why would I mind?"

Tony nodded. "Right. I keep forgetting you've taken yourself out of circulation. How's it going, anyhow? Is the famous Brannan charm cutting any ice with Kelly Flynn?"

"Yes and no," Jed answered, handing Tony a cup. "Have you brought the blueprints?" He didn't want to get involved in explaining to his friend—even his best friend—that Kelly said she loved him, seemed to love him, yet for two weeks had left him with the uneasy sense that something was wrong, something more than her reluctance to marry. "I'm afraid I have to leave town within the hour," he said by way of apology for his abruptness. "There's trouble with the Baffin Island project."

"Serious?" Tony asked, taking the blueprints from a cardboard tube and unrolling them on Jed's desk.

"Serious enough. Sloppy bureaucrats shipped the wrong materials to the site so the workers—premium-priced workers, by the way—are sitting around getting antsy, and the supervisor's talking about quitting."

"Well, the construction company involved is only a subsidiary of yours. Why do you have to go, Jed? Why not send its president?"

"He's away on another emergency, and every hour counts, especially in the north. Workers, weather, transportation . . . it all has to come together or the whole thing goes right down the tube."

"Okay," Tony said. "I know what you're up against. There are just a couple of things I want to check with you about the plans for the house."

The house, Jed thought as he and Tony went over the blueprints, the dream house he and Kelly had talked about during long walks on the beach years ago. It would be a multilevel, natural-wood hideaway with cathedral ceilings and big open rooms with lots of fireplaces. Poised on a point of land overlooking the water, it would be lined on its lakefront side with windows and a sundeck.

The house soon would be a reality, but the dream seemed to be slipping away, and Jed didn't know why. He and Kelly loved each other. They had fun together. Yet as soon as they'd been apart even for a day, she was preoccupied and withdrawn. He wanted to blame her work load; she certainly was tired. What was wrong?

"Jed?"

He gave himself a mental shake, suddenly aware Tony was staring at him exactly the way Diane had earlier. "Sorry," he mumbled. "I've got too much on my mind, I guess." Forcing himself to pay attention, he managed to answer all Tony's questions without further lapses.

Tony rolled up the blueprints. "One more thing," he said, inserting the roll into the tube. "Those long narrow windows in the master bedroom—the ones up near the ceiling. How about using stained glass for them?"

Jed thought about the possibility and wondered why it hadn't occurred to him. "Perfect," he said, imagining the sun filtering through the jewel colors of a Celtic symbol to cast a glow over the bed. "But Kelly's swamped as it is."

"It doesn't have to be done right away; we'll put in ordinary panes for the time being, but think about the stained glass. It's the kind of challenge Kelly Flynn would love, in my opinion. And it would be hers instead of something she was doing for a stranger."

"She doesn't know about the house." The more Jed thought about the idea the better he liked it, but there were problems in the way. "How could she do the job well without seeing the windows and at least the framework of the room?"

Tony was ready with a solution. "Leave the details to me. Kelly doesn't have to know whose house it is. I assume you'll want her to use Celtic themes."

"Definitely," Jed answered. "But be sure Kelly doesn't feel any sort of pressure at all. Your mystery client has to be very easygoing, make no demands."

Tony gulped down his coffee. "I know, I know. I'll tell Kelly she's doing the windows for some eccentric New York tycoon who happened to see her work in a gallery and doesn't care if he has to wait months or even years for the end result."

"Eccentric?" Jed repeated, getting to his feet as Tony rose and started for the door.

"You're asking me to build a house as a surprise for the woman you plan to marry, and you're not sure she's going to cooperate. You'll hire her to do stained-glass windows for her own bedroom—assuming she actually will move into the place—and you're not telling her she's ultimately her own client. Eccentric? Why would I call you eccentric?"

"The stained-glass windows were your idea."

Tony merely grinned and put his hand on the door-knob. "I can't figure it," he mused. "How does a man fall so hard for one particular woman? You've invested a lot in Kelly Flynn, Jed, and I'm not talking about money. What if she won't marry you?"

"She'll marry me," Jed stated. "If I have to kidnap her until she . . . well, until I break down her resistance, that's exactly what I'll do."

"Careful, pal. You're living in the wrong era by at least a few hundred years, if not a few thousand. Tossing the woman of your choice over your shoulder and carrying her off to your Viking ship has been frowned on for quite a while now."

Jed laughed. Tony's expression during his little lecture was serious. "I was kidding, for Pete's sake."

"I'm not so sure," Tony said as he opened the door and made a beeline for Diane.

Jed wasn't so sure himself. All he needed was time with Kelly, time to get her used to having him around again, time to earn all her trust, time to court her in the old-fashioned way she deserved. At the moment, however, time was the one thing he didn't have.

He picked up the phone and tried to call her once more. His heart beat wildly when he didn't get a busy signal. After three rings someone answered. "Is Kelly Flynn there by any chance?" Jed asked, hoping his luck had changed.

"I'm sorry, but she just left," a pleasant woman said. "And I don't know where she was going from here. She has an answering machine at her home, so if you wanted to phone there and leave a message she'd get back to you."

"Thanks," Jed murmured. "That's what I'll have to do." He made the call and explained on Kelly's machine what had happened and why he had to make his trip, but hung up depressed. He had the sinking feeling he wouldn't be greeted with open arms when he came back home.

By noon he was on his way to Baffin Island, wondering again what had happened to his Irish luck.

Kelly picked up her messages a few minutes after noon and felt cheated; if only she'd checked her machine earlier she could have wished Jed a safe journey. She could have assured him that she understood business problems. He had sounded so sad and concerned during his explanation.

His voice, she thought, so deep and rich. Not at all like the thin singsong one that taunted her every day and night—and lately at three and four in the morning, giving her a rude, terrifying awakening.

Except when Jed was with her.

She couldn't accept the possibility that Jed was her caller, or had arranged for someone else to do the phoning. Sneakiness, bullying, and obscenity weren't his style. Kelly smiled at the understatement. Sneaks, bullies, and obscene callers didn't even seem part of the same world Jed Brannan existed in.

No, Jed wasn't the culprit in this little mystery. It was someone else, someone who knew when she was alone. Someone, therefore, who was watching her.

An underlying dread had begun to permeate Kelly's every moment, waking or sleeping—and she slept very little these days. If the harassment didn't stop soon, she didn't know how she could keep going. Exhaustion was getting harder and harder to fight, and a debilitating, constant depression was settling over her. She didn't know what to do. The police couldn't help her; their only advice was to get an unlisted number. It was quickly becoming her only alternative, but she didn't kid herself into believing it would do much good. Too many people had to have access to the number. Even getting a separate business phone and an unlisted private one wouldn't help, because her seamstresses called her at all sorts of odd hours, so she'd have to pick up the business line anyway. It wouldn't take her pervert long to figure that out.

Tell Jed, a small voice nagged her. *Turn to him, trust him.*

Kelly had fought the urge to go to Jed with the problem. Her independence, so precious and hard won, was already undermined by her love for him. She found herself adjusting schedules to make time to be with him. She felt an electric excitement building in her when she knew she was going to see him. She liked his attitude of protectiveness toward her, yet she scolded herself constantly for lapsing into such typically feminine responses.

But now that Jed was out of town and she couldn't run to him for help even if she wanted to, she felt abandoned and vulnerable.

Stiffening her resolve, she reminded herself that if Jed hadn't come back into her life, she would have found a way to solve her problem on her own. The solution was simple—fight back.

There were countless calls that night. Kelly engaged in a duel with her tormentor, refusing to listen to a single word the singsong voice had to say. She didn't hide behind her answering machine, but took every call herself and hung up the instant she heard the hated voice. It grew more shrill with each attempt to make her listen, and she knew she might be courting trouble. The man might get mad enough to come after her.

"Let him," she muttered as she worked feverishly in her studio, taking calls with her left hand and sketching Christmas ornament designs with her right. She was frightened, but, even more, she was angry. An open battle was better than guerrilla warfare. Maybe, just maybe, the bully would get bored with the whole exercise and give up on her.

The phone was silent for the first hour after midnight, and Kelly was tempted to go to bed. Instead she made herself a big pot of coffee. It was better to stay up all night than to be wakened by threats and obscenities.

The calls began again at three and lasted, at fifteen-minute intervals, until five. Kelly braced herself at five-fifteen, but the phone remained silent. At five-thirty, nothing again. By six, she knew she'd outlasted her enemy, at least for this night. Even he had to sleep sometime.

Crawling into bed Kelly fell asleep immediately, despite the coffee she'd poured into herself, and was almost refreshed when she got up at ten.

The sky at the horizon was dull, and the television weatherman reported a storm brewing over the Great Lakes. It would hit the Traverse Bay region within hours . . . a day or two, at most. The weatherman warned against high winds and treacherous waters, even issued a tornado watch: Kelly felt her body tensing up, her old, superstitious fears resurfacing. She stepped into the shower and let the hot water beat down on the back of her neck, vowing she'd fight this battle too. It was time to grow up. There were no banshees. She didn't believe in little people and pots of gold at the end of rainbows, so why give in to irrational fears of supernatural creatures foretelling death? She didn't even know where she'd picked up that silliness, certainly not from her parents. She'd probably heard talk beside a campfire while ghost stories made the rounds. She'd been such an impressionable child, it was no wonder some of the tales had left their mark. *Banshees indeed. Utter rubbish,* she told herself.

The day went more smoothly than most, as if to prove to Kelly that her positive attitude was affecting events. The next was even better, with seamstresses completing projects in record time and another major quilt sold from a Mackinac Island shop and, best of all, a new stained-glass assignment from Tony Leonard. She looked forward to that particular challenge, eagerly anticipating the meeting with Tony at the house he was building for a client who wanted Celtic-motif stained-glass windows.

Kelly missed Jed but otherwise was feeling pleased with the way things were going. She had even summoned the courage to thwart her anonymous caller by letting her machine take all messages until midnight and then simply unplugging the phone. His recorded threats escalated with his frustration; he'd even begun suggesting that if she wouldn't talk to him by phone, she'd have to face him in person, but Kelly gambled on his cowardice—and kept a cast-iron frying pan by her bed. She slept fitfully, but she did sleep.

The storm hit with awesome force on the third night after Jed had left. Kelly played a tape of Wagner's *Ride of the Valkyries* at full volume, thumbing her nose at supernatural death messengers, while she put the finishing touches to the design for Beauregarde's stained-glass portrait.

Then the power went out.

Plunged into utter blackness and a silence shattered only by the wind's screams, Kelly battled her rising panic. She felt her way from the studio to the kitchen, then groped in a drawer for a candle and some matches.

Shakily she stuck one end of the candle into a holder and lit the match. The wick resisted the flame at first but finally caught. Kelly's initial relief was short-lived. As she saw the eerie shadows flickering on the walls she wondered if total darkness would have been less nerve-racking.

A cup of tea would calm her, she told herself, and was about to fill the kettle when she remembered that she needed electricity to operate the stove.

If ever there was a time to keep working, she decided, this was it. She carried the candle to her studio, refusing to allow her imagination to dwell on the unknown terrors lurking in dark corners of her cottage.

When the phone rang a few minutes later, her first thought was that it was Jed. *Please let it be Jed,* she said silently. As she reached for the receiver, a second possibility occurred to her . . . a far more likely possibility. She hesitated. Answer it? Or leave it? she wondered.

By the tenth ring, Kelly knew who was calling. Wishing her answering machine were battery-operated instead of plugged into the wall, she decided at last to pick up the receiver and deal with the caller in a sane, rational manner, no matter what he said to her.

"Do you hear them?" the thin voice whined as soon as Kelly had put the receiver to her ear. "Hear the banshees, Kelly Flynn?" A click. The line went dead.

Kelly replaced the receiver very slowly, her hands shaking, her mind whirling. Only one person knew about her superstitious fear. Only one person knew how she connected the sound of the wind with the wail of the banshees. Only one person.

Eight

Jed drove straight to Kelly's place as soon as he hit Traverse City. Surely she'd be home, he told himself. It was after ten at night. He knew he should call first, but he couldn't wait. He'd taken a tortuous route through Montreal and Detroit just to get back a day early. The business project was back on track: Now he wanted to be sure he hadn't messed up what mattered most to him.

As he approached her cottage he saw her lights were on. She was home and she was awake. He could hardly believe that after five days of missing her, of wondering what she was thinking, he was finally going to see her and talk to her.

Kelly heard the car motor and glanced out the window long enough to see the headlights of a car as it turned into her driveway. Grabbing her iron frying pan she made a dash for the front door and pressed herself against the wall beside it. For two days the thin voice on her answering machine had been hurling threats at her. For two days she'd been waiting, braced. She'd called the police, and they'd taken a tape in the faint hope of getting a match on a voice print. A squad car drove by occasionally and paused outside her house, but it was small comfort when Kelly was being given accounts of her every move for the past six hours by the caller. She wanted to unplug the phone, wanted to ignore the words that were enunciated so clearly into her answering machine while she sat staring, listening. "You're completely alone," she'd heard repeatedly, like a chant. "So isolated in your little cottage, Kelly. The banshees tried to warn you, but you wouldn't listen. I'm coming for you, Kelly Flynn. Very soon. But not when the police are there. I can wait until you're alone."

She heard the car door slam, then the crunch of footsteps on gravel. If only she dared to peek outside. Perhaps it was the police, breaking the schedule they'd established. Or perhaps one of her seamstresses was dropping by. Even as she formed the thought she knew it was nonsense.

Kelly clutched the handle of the frying pan, wondering if she should have arranged to get a gun. But she didn't know how to go about doing it, didn't know how to use one, and was sure she'd panic in the crunch. A frying pan was more her speed. She might not be capable of shooting a man, but she'd bop him on the head without a moment's hesitation.

The three steps on her front porch creaked one after the other. Then there were three sharp raps on the door. Kelly scowled, a little taken aback. Did attackers usually knock?

Her anonymous caller was a nut, she decided grimly. He might do anything, and he knew she was alone—he'd pointed it out often enough. He'd knock just to build the suspense.

She tightened her grip on the pan and remained pressed against the wall, feeling like a rabbit in a hole with a great paw reaching in after her. She was tempted to wait, to hope the man outside would go away, but her temper was building. She'd had it with being victimized. After putting up a strong front, she wasn't going to shrink from it now. It was time to confront her enemy. Anything was better than the torture she'd been enduring.

Letting go of the pan with one hand, she reached across the door and released the locks, then turned the knob and threw the door wide open, staying behind it and using it as a shield as she gripped her makeshift weapon in her two hands and raised it over her head.

Jed took one step inside the cottage and frowned. "Kelly?" he said, puzzled. She'd opened the door, but where was she?

Kelly froze, then let the weapon slip from her hands and clatter to the floor behind her as she threw herself against Jed, wrapping her arms around his neck until she nearly strangled him.

At first Jed was thrilled with the enthusiasm of the greeting, but he couldn't help noticing the metallic clang of the iron frying pan that was wobbling noisily to a stop on the floor. When he felt the convulsive trembling of her body, he finally realized something was very wrong. "What's going on here?" he demanded, alarmed.

Kelly realized with a start what she'd done. All her feisty independence had disappeared the instant she'd set eyes on Jed. She'd completely forgotten the evidence pointing to him as her villain, her whole being responding to his reassuring presence with joy and relief.

She moved away from him and picked up the pan, trying to seem casual. "Nothing," she answered in a tiny voice. "I—I just dropped this, that's all."

"You were going to the door with an iron frying pan

in your hands and there's nothing going on," Jed stated in a monotone.

"You caught me as I was about to cook something."

"At ten o'clock?"

"Late supper," she explained lamely.

"That's why you were holding the pan over your head when I walked through the door. What were you planning to cook? Scrambled brains? I have a feeling I'm lucky not to be lying on the floor with my head bashed in."

Kelly took the pan to the kitchen and put it in the cupboard, stuck for an answer.

Jed followed her. "I've had it, Kelly. Something's going on here. Something's been going on here for a while, and you're going to tell me what it is."

She leaned against the cupboard and studied him. He looked tired. He also looked as if he might pick her up and shake the information out of her if she didn't explain. Was it possible Jed was her caller? Even the evidence she'd heard with her own ears hadn't convinced her he was. There had to be some explanation for the banshee remarks. She was incapable of believing that this man, whose big, solid body made her feel so warm and safe, whose face was so expressive of his every emotion, whose eyes blazed with concern and love, could do anything to hurt her. "It's . . . some annoying phone calls," she said at last.

Jed's eyes narrowed. "What kind of phone calls?"

Kelly shrugged. "Obscene, basically."

"What do you mean 'basically'?"

She chewed on her lower lip. "Well . . . he's been adding some . . . threats. I provoked it. I wouldn't listen to him any more, so he got mad and started saying he'd"—her voice trailed off until it was barely audible— "he'd get me."

Jed stared at her, the muscle in his jaw working, his

hands clenched into fists. "How long have you been putting up with this?"

"A few weeks," Kelly mumbled. It struck her how completely Jed dominated her small kitchen. It wasn't just his size that created such an overpowering effect. There was a whole aura of commanding height and breadth about him, as if the force of his personality were a palpable, physical thing. She headed off his next question. "I didn't tell you because . . . I wanted to handle the problem myself. And I thought it would stop eventually."

"Is this why you've seemed so tired?" he asked quietly.

Kelly nodded. "He started phoning late at night. I haven't been getting a lot of sleep, I guess."

"But you wouldn't tell me." Jed was annoyed and puzzled and still not sure she was being fully honest. He studied her tense face, the wariness in her eyes. "The calls started, then, not long before I first contacted you. And you received one tonight before I arrived, one that frightened you very badly." He went to her and cradled her face in his hands, making her look at him. "Did you think I had something to do with it, Kelly?"

She averted her gaze.

"Look at me, Kelly. And answer me."

"There was a storm," she finally whispered. "An awful storm. He called . . ." Kelly drew a shaky breath and looked into Jed's penetrating gray eyes. "He told me to listen to the banshees."

Jed's expression was sad and searching. "So somehow he knew about that, and he obviously never called while I was with you—which on its own might have made you wonder. And what better way to drive you into my arms than by making you afraid to be alone?"

Kelly said nothing. Those were the facts that had been plaguing her.

"Then why," Jed asked softly, "did you drop your crazy weapon and fly at me as if I'd arrived to save you?"

"Because you had," Kelly blurted. "That—that monster had just phoned and threatened me. He said I was all alone and he was right, except that when I thought he was coming after me it turned out to be you, so I . . ." Kelly's eyes filled with tears and she turned her face so her lips pressed against his palm. "I wasn't alone anymore," she whispered.

Jed folded his arms around her, his rising anger at her tormentor blunted for the moment by the joy she'd given him. Buried under all her layers of fear was a foundation of trust in him that nothing had managed to crack. Now that he knew it existed, he would build on it. "No, sweetheart," he murmured against the fragrant softness of her hair. "You're not alone anymore."

Kelly didn't even try to fight the feeling of safety being in Jed's arms gave her. She could and would fight her own battles, but for the moment she was glad she didn't have to.

"You're so tired, Kelly. You need sleep. And to tell the truth, so do I."

Kelly looked up and realized how drawn and exhausted Jed seemed. "Was it a rough trip?"

"Hectic. Frustrating. The problems got solved, but it was like pulling teeth all the way. And the whole time I kept wondering whether you felt I'd broken my promise."

"What promise?" Kelly asked, frowning in puzzlement.

"I said I was here to stay. Two weeks later I'm taking off without even getting a chance to explain why in person."

Kelly smiled, stood on tiptoe, and kissed the tiny cleft in Jed's chin. "I didn't think you meant you'd never leave Traverse City at all. I'm not that immature, you know."

"You're not immature at all, Kelly. You're a strong, beautiful, incredible woman, and I love you more than I knew I could love anyone." He lowered his head and captured Kelly's lips in a gentle kiss that gradually deepened and intensified until they were both breathless. "I'll show you how much I love you," Jed added. "I'll take you to bed and hold you all night so you can sleep. Nothing more. I'll just hold you close."

Kelly laughed huskily. "I'm . . . ah . . . I'm not that tired, Brannan. If *you* are, of course . . ."

"I'll never be that tired," he murmured. "Especially when I haven't been able to make love to you for five days."

"Six," she corrected him. "We weren't together the night before you left, but who's counting?"

Another car pulled into the driveway, the headlights illuminating Jed's car.

His body was instantly coiled for action. "I'll see who that is," he muttered, releasing Kelly and heading for the door.

She watched him for a moment, then picked up her frying pan. It never hurt to be prepared for the worst.

Jed opened the front door, and Kelly moved in behind him with pan at the ready.

"Jed?" A man's voice queried. "Is that you?"

Jed relaxed, recognizing the policeman, an old friend. "It's me, Terry. What are you doing here?"

"Kelly Flynn's been having some troublesome phone calls. We've been checking in on her whenever we could. Has there been any trouble?"

"I got here a few minutes ago. The guy never calls her when I'm around, so I don't imagine he'll show up either. Thanks for looking in on her."

"Any time. Wish we could do more for the lady, but these anonymous callers are hard to track down. Usually they're more of a nuisance than a real danger, but

I'm glad you're here, Jed. Kelly's pretty vulnerable if the guy does turn out to be dangerous."

"I'm going to take care of that particular problem," Jed stated firmly. "She won't stay alone here another minute. Thanks again, Terry." Closing the door, Jed turned and was startled to find Kelly right behind him, scowling and wielding her chunk of cast iron. "That's my girl," he said with an affectionate smile. "We'll go back-to-back and take on all comers, right?"

Kelly looked at her weapon and gave a little shrug. "Well, you never know. . . . Was that Terry MacKay?"

Jed nodded, gently taking the frying pan from Kelly's hand and placing it on the counter. "You heard our conversation?"

"What was that you said about how you're going to take care of 'that particular problem,' about how I wouldn't stay alone here another minute?"

"We'll discuss it tomorrow, sweetheart." Jed secured the door's locks. "Right now, you go get ready for bed. I'll make you something to drink and then get the lights."

Kelly put her hands on her hips and shot him a slightly challenging look. "If I'm such a mature, strong woman, why are you trying to tell me what to do?"

Jed kissed the top of her head. "I'm not trying to tell you. I'm telling you. Why? I'm bigger than you, that's why."

Kelly thought she should argue with him, but wasn't in the mood. "You've got a point there," she conceded, then made a halfhearted effort at stubbornness. "Exactly what are we going to discuss tomorrow?"

"Many things," Jed answered cheerfully. He grasped her shoulders and turned her in the direction of the bedroom. "What'll it be? Tea?" He kissed the back of her neck in fond remembrance of what *tea* had meant to them that first night. "Or perhaps a nightcap? Hot chocolate?"

"Hot chocolate would be nice," Kelly said softly, melting at his touch and the warmth of his breath against her skin. She decided that going straight to bed was an excellent plan.

As she undressed she heard Jed working in the kitchen, whistling and opening cupboard doors. "I use instant mix," she called out to him. "Second cupboard to the right of the fridge, bottom shelf."

"Got it," he said a moment later, then resumed his whistling. Kelly didn't recognize the tune; Jed seemed to be making it up as he went along.

Kelly smiled contentedly, reaching into a dresser drawer for the new little confection she'd stashed there, a peach teddy that was all satin and lace. She felt a bit self-conscious as she slipped into it; deliberate seductiveness was new to her.

When Jed walked into the room a few minutes later and nearly dropped the tray he was carrying, Kelly's confidence rose by several degrees.

"Nice," he said quietly, his voice a little thick. He managed to put the tray on the night table, then stood by the bed looking down at Kelly. "Nice," he repeated.

Kelly's body responded to his gaze as it slowly, lovingly caressed her. She felt no shyness, only delight at having pleased Jed, at making his eyes darken to black velvet, his voice take on the husky timbre that signaled his desire. "I missed you, Brannan," she told him unashamedly. "And I do love you."

Then marry me, Jed wanted to say, *stop fighting me, fighting us.* But for a change he curbed his impatience. "I know," he replied, smiling. "I know it more tonight than ever." He began undressing, his eyes never straying from their slow perusal of Kelly's delectable form. "Drink your hot chocolate," he suggested as he unbuttoned his shirt.

With catlike grace Kelly slid to a sitting position and reached for the cup. She took a sip, watching Jed's every move. "Mmmm," she said.

"You like it?" he asked, undoing his belt.

"It's wonderful." She took another sip. "And the hot chocolate's good too."

Jed laughed as he stripped off his remaining clothes. "I love the way you leer," he murmured.

"Leer? Is that what I'm doing?"

"I'd like to think so, sweetheart."

Kelly nodded. "I'm leering, definitely leering. But you're so"—she sighed happily—"so leerable."

Jed stretched out beside her, propping his head up on his elbow and continuing to look at Kelly, enjoying the view too much to be in a hurry, though he knew the next view would be even better. "And you're so lovable," he said. "You know what I'm going to do someday? I'm going to compile a dictionary of Kellyisms."

"Now you're doing it yourself—making up words. See how easy it is? How convenient?" With Jed so close, Kelly's interest in her hot chocolate waned. She tried to finish it quickly.

"Take your time," he told her. "Some things should be savored. Hot chocolate's one of them." He reached out to tug on a thin satin ribbon at the valley between her breasts. The tiny bow came undone, releasing the soft mounds that had been peeking through the pale lace. "And you, Kelly-love," he added, cupping one creamy globe, "are another."

A shiver of excitement coursed through her. "And when do I get to savor you?" she asked in a shaky voice.

Jed lowered one silk spaghetti strap, smiling with the inner happiness of a man absorbed in a delightful endeavor. "I've already told you that," he answered. "For the rest of our lives." Leaning toward her, he tasted the delicate floral bouquet of her throat and shoulder.

Kelly was acutely aware of how the atmosphere of the night had changed dramatically, how the simple fact of Jed's arrival had transformed fear and exhaustion and misery into complete bliss.

He teased her mercilessly. "Drink your chocolate," he ordered with feigned gruffness when she grew too excited, her body demanding fulfillment. It was a loving game she couldn't lose, and he couldn't help winning.

By the time the chocolate was gone, Kelly was a twisting, dancing flame that flared out of control at Jed's every touch and kiss.

At last he filled her with himself. Kelly gasped with the intensity of the sensation and dug her fingers into Jed's shoulders, holding on as something deep inside her exploded and a thousand shooting stars fanned out in the universe of her mind. She smoothed her hands over the hot, sleek muscles of his back as the stars drifted into nothingness, but suddenly she was racked by another thrusting, bursting rocket, and another and another. It was almost too wild an ecstasy to bear, but Jed held her and kissed her and she was safe again. "I love you, Jed," she whispered as she felt his body nearing its own release. "Dear heaven, I love you so, so much."

Jed's arms tightened around her as her heartfelt words thrilled him, made him soar upward with her, his whole being consumed by her fire.

They clung to each other, laughing softly from sheer joy, their bodies melded together as they slowly drifted back to earth.

Kelly was asleep minutes later, her lips curved in a smile as she nestled against Jed's chest.

Sleep didn't come to Jed as easily, despite his tiredness. His initial elation at Kelly's instinctive trust gave way to a more sobering thought: All this time she'd kept her troubles to herself. He recalled countless instances when she could have told him about the anonymous calls, when he'd asked her what was bothering her, why she was always tired. She'd sidestepped his queries like a politician at a news conference.

Kelly shifted slightly in her sleep, cuddling closer to Jed, her lips brushing his chest, her body as warm and relaxed as a child's.

He kissed her temple as a great wave of tenderness washed over him, yet he felt confused. Kelly was like two different people with him. One had thrown herself into his arms at the peak of her fear and in the face of damning evidence that he was her enemy. That Kelly was loving, trusting. That Kelly was happy to belong to him.

The other Kelly withheld her thoughts and was secretive about crucial events, clinging to her independence and shutting him out as if he were a stranger.

It was time, he decided grimly, to get to the bottom of a few things.

Nine

Kelly was smiling when she padded out to the kitchen, her hair still damp from her shower, her naked body wrapped in a yellow terry cloth robe. She was sure every inch of her glowed, inside and out, from the lovemaking that had started her day.

Her smile faded when she saw the obstinate set of Jed's jaw. He had showered first, leaving her to lounge in bed an extra few minutes. While she showered, he had come out to make coffee and see what he could find to eat.

She sat down at the tiny table in the corner of the kitchen and watched Jed as he placed a mug of steaming coffee in front of her and another at the place he'd set opposite hers. There were already a plate of buttered toast on the table and a tiny pot of strawberry jam. "What do you usually eat for breakfast?" he asked. "Your cupboards aren't exactly filled to capacity."

"I don't usually eat breakfast," she said.

"That's what I thought. And I'll bet you forget about lunch half the time, probably dinner as well. You don't take care of yourself at all, Kelly."

"I get along quite nicely, thank you," she said coolly, though she knew he was right. More often than not she forgot to eat until a headache and a spell of dizziness reminded her to. "If I'd known you were coming, I'd have baked a croissant," she added with a trace of sarcasm.

"I know," he shot back. "A store-bought croissant. I've stayed with you before, remember? I guess what you do for guests and what you do for yourself are two different things. Is any of the food in this house not frozen?"

"So I'm an inefficient homemaker," Kelly said. "And I support the frozen-food industry. So what? It's my business, one of the joys of living alone. It's also one very good reason why any man would be an idiot even to consider marrying me. I hardly can take care of myself, as you see, so how could I possibly take care of a husband?" She tore off a hunk of toast and bit into it violently.

"Did it ever occur to you," Jed said slowly, wishing he hadn't let his inner tension get the best of him, "that a husband might take care of you?"

Kelly stared at him, then picked up her mug and gulped her coffee. "We're back to that, are we?"

"You brought up the subject of husbands," Jed pointed out. "I didn't."

"Why are you suddenly so cranky?" Kelly asked in a small voice. "I was feeling really happy after our wonderful lovemaking, and then all of a sudden you're attacking me about frozen food."

Jed closed his eyes, sighed deeply, then looked at Kelly with an apologetic smile. "Our lovemaking *was* wonderful," he said gently. "I guess when I saw your empty shelves, I was struck with a sense of how alone you are, how alone you've been throughout this ordeal with that anonymous caller, and I got mad at you for not telling me." He shrugged. "So I picked on you about the frozen food. The truth is, I love frozen croissants."

"I'm sorry I was out of them," Kelly said as a peace offering . . . and as a way to divert the conversation.

"Toast is fine, your being alone isn't. You do realize it can't continue, don't you?"

"Are we about to discuss what you said to Terry MacKay last night? About what you called 'that particular problem'?" Kelly asked with a sigh of resignation.

"I'll give you a choice. I move in here, or you move into Kernaghan's place."

Kelly finished chewing her toast before answering him, then spoke in a low, controlled voice. "Being a great lover doesn't give you the right to offer me choices of that nature, Brannan."

"Maybe not, but I'm doing it anyway. Now, which is it to be? I vote for you moving into Kernaghan's house."

"It's your house now," Kelly said irrelevantly. "Why do you keep referring to it as Kernaghan's?"

Jed was lost for words for a moment; he hadn't noticed the slip. He also wasn't sure how to answer. The truth was that his grandfather's home wasn't his on a permanent basis. He had another house in mind when he thought of home. "It's hard to get used to new habits," he said at last. "But don't try to steer me away from the main point. I want you to move in there. There's a huge room on the third floor that isn't being used. I can set up a studio for you—it's even air-conditioned."

Kelly realized she wasn't feeling the heat as much as usual this morning. She glanced around and saw that the windows were open and the breeze coming off the lake was delicious. "This is lovely," she said softly. "I'd stopped opening the windows when I was alone after dark. I didn't think of it last night. When did you do it?"

"After you'd fallen asleep. I realized the place was hot and stuffy, and then I realized why. Which just confirms my point: You can't continue staying here alone."

Kelly stared off into space for a while, then blurted out the thought that was troubling her. "How did he know about the banshees?"

Jed reached across the table to take her hand in his. "Are you having second thoughts? Wondering if I'm really the culprit after all? Especially since I'm turning it to my advantage by insisting you stay with me?"

Kelly considered his question carefully. Why *had* she thought about the caller right at that point? Then she remembered the open windows. Because Jed was with her she could sleep with the fresh air wafting in through open windows. Because one man was tormenting her, she had to depend on another man for something as basic as fresh air. It was like a conspiracy. Anyone with half a brain would suspect Jed. "No," she told him honestly. "I'm not having second thoughts. If you were willing to do something illegal to get to me—which I'd have to be awfully conceited to believe—it wouldn't be slimy phone calls. You'd abduct me, seduce me, keep me until I gave in. Something more direct, honest in its arrogance. A forthright power play."

"I'm glad you have such faith in me," he said, wishing Kelly hadn't hit so close to the truth. He got up and walked around to stand behind her chair, idly lifting her soft, damp curls to dry them in the breeze. "You almost sound wistful," he teased. "As if you wish I'd do just that, take away your need to decide whether or not to give yourself, really give your whole self, to me. Perhaps it'd be easier for you if I simply spirited you away and made you all mine."

"Perhaps it would," Kelly mused in a voice just above a whisper.

Jed's hands drifted to her shoulders and tightened around them. "What did you say?"

Kelly gave her head a little shake. "I was kidding, Brannan. I've already told you I don't approve of strong-arm tactics." She smiled nervously.

But Jed had heard her words, and he wasn't about to be jollied into another good-natured verbal sparring match. What she'd said was too revealing to be glossed over. He leaned down and scooped her up in his arms. "I think you do go for strong-arm tactics, sweetheart. I think it's what you want from me."

An undeniable thrill raced through Kelly as he lifted her and walked out of the kitchen carrying her as if she were weightless. She couldn't help laughing from the surprise of his sudden move . . . and from the embarrassment of her impulsive confession. It was true that she wanted to drop all the barriers she'd erected between them over the years, but she couldn't seem to do it. More than once she'd caught herself dreaming that Jed would crash right through them. He'd already come close by driving out her fears with the intoxicating drug of his lovemaking.

Her body tingled at the prospect of more of his touches and kisses, more of him filling her. Time meant nothing, work meant nothing, reality meant nothing to her.

She was faintly disappointed when Jed took her to the couch instead of the bedroom, but when he sat down and cuddled her on his lap she took advantage of the situation, nuzzling into his throat, her tongue darting out to lick his freshly-showered skin. "I love the taste of you," she said with her lips against him. "When you wear cologne, you're delicious, but without it, when it's just your own lovely scent . . . mmm."

Jed was determined that they talk, but he was sorely tempted by Kelly's uninhibited sensuality. Now that she was getting to know him physically, intimately, she was learning his weaknesses. She knew exactly how to make him forget everything but his constant, driving need for her. "Listen, brat," he said raggedly. "We have some decisions to make."

Her fingers inched inside his shirt, then deftly undid a button. Her lips trailed downward as she opened a few more buttons.

Jed shuddered, and his hand, seemingly of its own accord, parted her robe and cupped one softly-rounded breast. Groaning, he realized the balance of power had tilted in Kelly's direction, and he had only himself to blame: he'd taught her the effectiveness of love play.

With a supreme effort of will he removed his hand from her breast, closed her robe, and caught her lips in a hard kiss. He ground his mouth against hers and probed inside with deep thrusts of his tongue until he felt her whole body soften in response. Lifting his head, he saw her heavy-lidded expression and laughed quietly. "You learn too quickly, sweetheart. It scares me to think how you'll be able to twist me around your little finger after a few years of practice. But I still have a few shreds of sanity left. And Kelly, we are going to talk. Right now. You sit right here on my lap—and sit still!"

"Or what?" she challenged him, her lips curved in a knowing smile. She loved hearing the desperation in his voice. He was determined to be firm, but he was so close to losing control completely. With Jed Brannan around, it was fun being female, she realized. He was endearingly susceptible to her feminine wiles.

He recognized her triumphant expression: he'd worn one like it himself more than once. "Or I'll turn you over my knee," he told her.

Kelly smiled seductively. "That has interesting possibilities, Brannan. I didn't know you were into that sort of thing, but I'm willing to give it a try."

He tried to glare at her but couldn't keep the twinkle out of his eyes. "I've created a monster," he muttered. Then he had an inspiration. "There's always a cold shower. That works wonders. I happen to know from personal experience. Right, a cold shower." He started to get up, holding Kelly in his arms.

"We'll talk," she said hastily. She hated cold showers. Even on hot days she used hot water, and she had no doubt that Jed would make good on his threat.

"You'll behave?" he demanded. "No more nibbling and licking and . . . the rest of it?"

"I'll be the model of decorum," Kelly promised, though she dreaded the discussion she knew was coming. Still, she dreaded a cold shower more, and having a talk with Jed—an honest one—was inevitable.

Jed settled back onto the couch, keeping Kelly on his lap, but shifting her position to reduce the intensity of his temptation. Her warm body was playing havoc with his determination.

Kelly was fully aware of his discomfort, but played the innocent. "So what do you want to talk about, Jed?"

"Let's start with why you didn't tell me about the calls."

Kelly sighed and rested her head on Jed's shoulder as he cuddled her, his arms encircling her, his big hand warm and solid on her hip. She twined one arm around his neck and rested her other hand on his chest. "I knew what would happen if I told you," she finally answered. "I knew you'd never let me stay alone if you found out about those calls, and I wasn't ready for you to move in on me . . . or to insist I move to your place."

"You're sure it wasn't that you suspected me?"

"Well, it crossed my mind, naturally, especially when—" She sat up and looked at Jed, frowning. "How do you suppose he did know about the banshees? Do you think this place could be bugged? And why would anyone do that? Isn't it going a bit far for a telephone pervert to use electronic eavesdropping devices on his victims?"

"Beats me," Jed replied. "But I'll have the cottage checked just in case."

"Isn't that expensive? I mean, I can't afford to hire an electronics expert, and I won't let you pay for it."

Jed reached up and cupped his hand behind Kelly's head and gently brought it down to his shoulder. "Try not to be such a dope, will you? I'll have the house swept for devices, and I'll pay for it, and you have nothing to say about it. Anyway, I have a friend in the business. He'll give me a good deal."

"I'll pay you back," Kelly insisted.

Jed ignored her. "Is there anyone else who could know how those old banshee stories bothered you?"

"I suppose," Kelly recalled aloud, "my fears probably showed when the stories made the rounds at campfires, but that was years and years ago."

"What about Michael?"

Kelly sat up again. "What about him?" she asked sharply.

"He'd remember your superstitions."

"My brother would never do a thing like this," Kelly cried. She started to scramble away from Jed, but he held her in place. "Obviously Kernaghan told you about Mike's wild period, but that's over. He wouldn't do it, Brannan. Don't even suggest it."

"I'm not suggesting anything," he said calmly. "But I

do think it's possible that he might have mentioned his sister's superstitions to one of his cronies during that wild period of his. He hung around with some pretty weird characters, I understand."

Kelly decided she could relax again, so she snuggled back into Jed's arms. "I hadn't thought of that. I suppose it's a possibility. Did you know how much your grandfather helped Mike, by the way? How he became for him the—I guess you'd call it authority figure—that Michael seemed to crave after we'd lost our folks?"

Jed chuckled. "Kernaghan wrote me that he'd told Mike to shape up and start acting like a man instead of making life harder for his sister."

"Is that what he said?" Kelly asked, smiling. "Really?"

"Dorothy corroborates the story. She says Mike was furious, but Kernaghan offered to take him outside and straighten him out. The kid was so stunned that a seventy-odd-year-old man would make such a threat—and look perfectly capable of going through with it—he backed right down. He also broke down, Dorothy told me. Cried it all out, all the anger and the fear and the guilt . . ."

"Why should Michael feel guilty?"

"Because he was alive and his parents weren't. Because he was overwhelmed by the idea that he couldn't take care of himself, much less you. Because you were so strong while he was so weak."

"He wasn't weak. He was young, that's all."

"I know that and you know that, but Mike didn't know it."

"Kernaghan was there for us again," Kelly said softly. "I loved that man, Jed, and I was scared when he died. I felt as if Michael and I had been orphaned again. Mike's fine now, but then I didn't know how he'd react."

"Kernaghan did leave a terrible void," Jed said quietly. "I loved him too. I still do. I look at his picture, though, and feel as if he hasn't gone far."

"You're wise to do that, keep his picture around. I broke down every time I saw a photograph of my folks, so I put them all in albums and hid the albums away. I've never been able to take them out and look at them."

"Is that how you handle your emotions?" Jed asked, beginning to understand why Kelly shrank from commitment. "Are you hiding them away?"

Kelly said nothing for a long while. "Maybe," she murmured at last.

"What feelings frighten you most, sweetheart?"

Kelly realized after several minutes that she had a whole list of feelings she'd made a habit of suppressing, from missing her parents to loving Jed. At the thought, a shadow passed through her mind, a fear that left a coldness in its wake. "I don't know," she said with an embarrassed, strained laugh. "It's too well hidden, I guess. And I don't want to talk about this anymore."

Jed's arms tightened around her. "Okay, love. Let's discuss more practical issues. How does your day look? In terms of your schedule, that is."

"Not too bad, actually. The stores have enough goods to see them through the summer, and my people are working to get the fall and winter lines ready. I use these slower periods for my own projects, special quilt designs and stained-glass work, mostly. Do you know Tony Leonard?"

Jed nodded. "He's a friend of mine," he answered truthfully, knowing what was coming and hoping Kelly wouldn't put her facts together and guess his surprise. "Why do you ask, sweetheart? Do I have reason to be jealous?"

"Of Tony? Hardly. He's attractive but . . . I don't

know. I was never interested in him. But I *am* interested in the projects he throws my way. I'm supposed to see him tomorrow about doing some stained-glass panels for a house he's building. Can you believe it? The client wants Celtic-motif designs. I can hardly wait to sink my teeth into this project." She grinned at Jed. "Maybe you can help with ideas, since you've made such a study of the subject."

"Love to," Jed said quietly, beginning to feel guilty. He didn't like deception even when it was for a worthy cause, but he was glad Kelly was so excited about the assignment. "All the more reason for you to move to the house. Your little spare room is too small for such a big job."

Kelly raised her head and looked at him quizzically. "How did you know it was a big job? Did I say it was?"

Jed knew he had to make a quick recovery. "I assumed it was big. Otherwise Tony wouldn't act as go-between and make arrangements while he's building the house. He'd tell his client to go to a gallery or call you." Satisfied that he'd come up with a valid explanation, Jed thought he'd be wise to go on the offensive. "I want to have your things moved as soon as possible. Today, if I can arrange it. You can pack a bag with the basic items you'll need while I make some calls. We can stick around here to supervise the move, and by tonight, with any luck, you'll be settled into your new digs."

"Hold on a minute!" Kelly cried. "I haven't even agreed to go, and you've got me moved before sundown!"

"I believe in getting things done without wasting time," he explained with a grin.

"I've noticed. But really, Jed . . . I'm not sure. I guess it seems old-fashioned of me, but I'm leery about moving in with you. Living with you."

"That's easily solved. Marry me. Make an honest man of Jed Brannan at last. Lord knows he's waited long enough."

"Why?" Kelly asked on an impulse. "Why, if you kept loving me the way you say you did, has it been seven whole years?"

"I've wondered the same thing myself. But when I go back over those years in my mind, it seems that every time I decided I had to try to win you back, I heard you were involved with someone else. I was traveling constantly and I didn't think I had the right to offer you an unstable life if you had a chance to be happy elsewhere. I'd work at forgetting you and bury myself in Kernaghan Explorations for another few months, usually in some godforsaken corner of the world where even Kernaghan's letters rarely reached me. Then, over the past few months, I found out you weren't seeing anyone, hadn't really been seeing anyone for quite a while. I started to hope again, and I asked Kernaghan about you often enough. He knew what was on my mind. He wrote and told me he thought you still cared for me . . . so here I am. Does your question mean you've accepted my proposal? You'll marry me?"

"No," Kelly answered without hesitation, surprising herself with her vehemence.

"Why not?"

"I'm not sure." The cold sensation gripped her again. "It has to do with those fears I keep hidden, I think. I can't marry you, Jed. I just can't."

"Will you try to face the fears eventually?" he asked, barely able to breathe as he waited for her answer.

At last she nodded. "I'll try, but I can't promise anything. Marriage to you terrifies me, absolutely terrifies me. And I don't feel comfortable about living with you."

"You can have your own room," Jed argued. "My

mother's room. She won't be using it this summer. Okay?"

Kelly hesitated. The offer was tempting, and if she refused, Jed would move into the cottage. "My own room?" she repeated.

"And a studio upstairs."

Kelly sighed "Trying to resist you is like trying to hold back a runaway steamroller," she muttered, and nestled against him feeling much happier than she cared to admit. "All right, you win," she conceded. "But before we get the job done . . ." She resumed her nibbling and kissing, and it was another full hour before Jed began to make the arrangements for her move.

Dorothy fussed over her like a mother hen when she heard about the anonymous caller. "You look so tired, Kelly," she said. "And thin too."

"She doesn't eat," Jed put in, setting Kelly's suitcase down and heading back outside to direct the movers he'd miraculously arranged for that very afternoon. "She's needed a keeper for some time," he said over his shoulder as a parting shot.

"Men," the housekeeper muttered fondly. "But in this case I believe Jed's right. You shouldn't have stayed in that cottage all by yourself when you were being threatened. I'm so glad he talked you into coming to stay with us, dear. I gather the movers have brought your business essentials?"

"My desk and drawing board and files," Kelly said apologetically, wondering how Dorothy felt about having drastic changes thrust upon her. "Jed says there's room on the third floor. I hope I'm not putting you out."

"Don't be silly, child. It's time that spare room was put to good use. And Caitlin's bedroom, as well. It's seemed so empty this year."

"Where is Jed's mother?" Kelly asked, realizing how much basic information she and Jed hadn't discussed. "And how did the loss of Kernaghan affect her?"

"She took it hard, of course, but she was lucky. A few months ago she met a lovely man, and they were married before Kernaghan passed away. Alex—that's Caitlin's husband—managed to make her loss bearable by being there for her." Dorothy led Kelly to the kitchen and began making coffee. "You needed that, too, dear. A broad shoulder can be such a comfort, and you were all alone after your parents died."

"I had Kernaghan," Kelly protested. Out of habit, a habit established so long ago Kelly couldn't recall when, she began helping Dorothy by putting out cups and arranging cookies on a plate. "Kernaghan gave me his broad shoulder when it mattered most. And he was there for Michael."

"That's not what I mean and you know it," Dorothy stated. "I mean the kind of broad shoulder Jed is offering."

"I noticed you refused some attractive proposals in favor of keeping your independence, Dorothy," she added.

The woman smiled. "Sean Patrick Kernaghan was no saint, and neither is his grandson, but they do make other men pale in comparison. Don't get me wrong, Kelly. I wasn't in love with that old rascal, making his meals and pining away for him, but I was happy being part of his family. None of those attractive offers seemed . . . attractive enough. Anyway, to get back to Caitlin, she and Alex are in Europe all summer, but she'll be thrilled that you're with us and seeing Jed again. She was always fond of you, though admittedly she was as adamant as your parents about you two breaking up until . . ." Dorothy stopped and hurried to the hall to direct the movers who'd come in with Kelly's large filing cabinet.

Kelly frowned, wishing the woman hadn't been interrupted. It wasn't difficult to fill in the rest of what Dorothy had started to say, however, and Kelly suddenly felt as if a burden had been lifted from her shoulders.

Why hadn't it occurred to her, she wondered, that Jed had been pressured by both their families? Her own parents had expressed doubts about the wisdom of an eighteen-year-old marrying anyone, much less a young man who had years of traveling and dedication to work ahead of him. Kernaghan, Caitlin Brannan— even Dorothy—the entire older generation had lectured her about going to college, about waiting to get married when she was more mature.

She hadn't listened, but Jed had. And now that she'd seen how immature her brother was at eighteen, and she'd done some lecturing of her own, she realized how right everyone had been.

For the first time she began to believe in Jed's love and in the hurt she'd caused him by refusing to understand. She began to accept the fact that he really had loved her all along, that he'd have come back much sooner if she'd left a door open. But she hadn't. She'd told him she would get over him, and she'd set out to do just that . . . without much success.

As she followed Dorothy up to the bedroom that would be hers temporarily, Kelly was overwhelmed and humbled by the sudden knowledge that she and Jed shared a special kind of love, a love that time and distance and utter stupidity hadn't destroyed.

She went through the motions of admiring the old-fashioned, cozy room and the four-poster she remembered from her childhood, a bed meant for a princess she'd thought then, envying Jed's mother. But her mind wasn't on her surroundings. She kept trying to chase down the elusive specter that was spoiling this beautiful moment, that wouldn't let her luxuriate in rediscovered love. It was like trying to grasp smoke. How could she destroy a fear that wouldn't come out from the furthest recesses of her mind to wage a fair fight?

Perhaps, she thought, if she ignored it, sat back and enjoyed the new happiness she'd found with Jed, the haunting terrors would go away.

Ten

Kelly worked contentedly in the studio Jed had set up for her, enjoying the luxury of space and light.

She was at the easel he'd insisted on buying for her, ensconced on a high stool with a back on it, also a gift from Jed. Every time he watched her working he seemed to come up with some new innovation or piece of furniture to make her life easier and more comfortable.

Putting the finishing touches to the last of the mock-ups of the Beauregarde portrait, Kelly cocked her head to one side, studied the colors for a moment, then decided to clean her paintbrushes.

"What's this?" Jed asked as he walked into the studio, casually draping his arm around Kelly's waist and kissing her temple.

"You must be psychic," she told him. "I was about to see whether you could come up here."

"Of course I'm psychic. Have you forgotten my gypsy period, my fortune-telling?"

With a wave of her head Kelly indicated the painting on the easel and two others on a nearby table. "See if your crystal ball tells you which of those designs is the one you want me to have done up in stained glass."

"You mean I finally get to see them?"

Kelly smiled. She hadn't let Jed peek until the last mock-up was ready. "Keep in mind that the finished product will be much richer. I've tried to give you a general idea of color and line. These are my three favorites of all the designs I tried. You choose the one you like best."

Jed examined the one on the easel at length, then moved to the table to view the others. "I had no idea so much work was involved."

"It isn't usually," Kelly told him truthfully. "This was special."

Jed was quiet for a while, overwhelmed by the dramatic impact of each design, amazed they could all be centered on the same subject and use similar colors, yet look so different. "Who'd have thought old Beau could be transformed into art?" he said at last, unable to express his emotions properly. "You've given that crazy bird, I don't know, dignity, perhaps. Stature. A certain . . . dash."

Kelly finished cleaning her brushes and moved to stand near Jed. "Those black feathers will be a lot more effective in stained glass," she explained with a frown.

"You actually want me to choose just one?" Jed asked. "They're all great."

Kelly was gratified by his enthusiasm. She'd wanted to please him. "Just one," she said lightly.

"Which do you think?" he asked.

"Oh, no, Brannan. This is your project. You're the client. You make the final decision."

"I like all three," he insisted, going to stand in front of the easel. "This one is more detailed than the others. Almost like a mosaic, I'd say. It's fascinating." He moved back to the table, stroking his chin thoughtfully. "This one on the left is bolder; the lines are more sweeping, the colors stark. It's the most stylized, even bordering on being abstract. It's great." He scowled and shook his head. "But the one on the right really captures Beauregarde in all his arrogant glory. I can almost see his feathers ruffling and that gold beak working as if he's dying to speak his mind. I'd swear those yellow wattles around his eyes are actually quivering the way they do when he's excited."

Kelly bit down on her lower lip, trying to contain her delight. Jed was saying all the right things, really understanding what she'd tried to achieve.

"Can't do it," he said at last.

Her bubble burst. Was he going to cancel the project? "Can't do what?"

"I can't choose just one. I'll have to buy all three."

Relieved, Kelly grinned. "Okay. I'll take that as the ultimate compliment. Now, which one?"

"I'm serious. I'd like all three."

"Let's try it this way, Jed. Which one would Kernaghan have picked?"

Jed thought about it, then shook his head "All three."

"But you have to make a choice."

"Why?"

Kelly frowned. "Well . . . I don't know. You just have to."

"Why not honor Kernaghan's last request in triplicate?"

"Have you any idea how much that would cost?" Even as she spoke she knew it was a stupid argument. She'd begun to realize how wealthy Jed had become. It daunted her a little; she wasn't used to people who had no worries about money. It didn't seem right somehow.

"The least I can do," Jed explained patiently, "is pay homage to the bird who comforted my grandfather in his old age. After all it was my grandfather who made it possible for me to afford such a gesture."

"Kernaghan never experienced old age," Kelly mused aloud. "But really, Jed. To order all three designs? I'm flattered. Enormously flattered. But you're letting your enthusiasm run amuck."

"My mind's made up."

"Where would you keep three stained-glass panels?"

"Easy. In the solarium with Beau. He'll think he's in mynah-bird heaven, surrounded by images of himself. What more could he ask, given his conceit? It'll give him a new lease on life. He hasn't been himself since Kernaghan left him, you know."

"Jed Brannan," Kelly said fondly, "I don't think you hate that bird as much as you pretend to. I think you have a soft spot for him."

"Nonsense. He's disgusting. But he was Kernaghan's, and he did provide me with an excuse for meeting with Kelly Flynn. I owe him."

Kelly moved toward Jed and slid her arms around his waist, resting her cheek against his chest, loving him more every minute. "I have a feeling you'd have found a way."

"Probably," he murmured, nuzzling his face into her fragrant brown hair. "But I'm glad I didn't have to. I honestly like what you've done with these designs, sweetheart. Your talent knocks me out. Now that you're working here and I actually see the process as well as the results, I'm more impressed than ever. By the way," he added as casually as he could, "have you met with Tony Leonard about the other stained-glass assignment you mentioned?" Jed knew she'd met with Tony, and at the house that would be hers some day soon, if all went well. But he played dumb. "It didn't fall through, did it?"

"Not at all," Kelly said. "It's just that I wanted to

finish Beauregarde's portrait before starting anything else, but I've been thinking about those windows. Any ideas?"

Jed brushed his lips over her forehead and temple, then nibbled on her earlobe. "Lots of them, sweetheart."

"I mean about the stained glass." Kelly scolded him without conviction, tipping back her head and closing her eyes, loving the feel of Jed's lips and tongue and warm breath on her skin.

"Oh, that." Jed's lips trailed across Kelly's jawline and down her throat to the scented hollow at its base. "I think we should snuggle up in bed tonight with some books and see what we come up with for inspiration. Erotic symbolism would be nice."

"I was thinking more along the lines of historical figures," Kelly said. "The High Kings, for instance. The windows are long and narrow and would really . . ." She hesitated as a shiver of delight raced through her. Jed traced the rounded dip of her red tank top with his tongue, giving special attention to the cleft between her breasts. "Would really lend themselves . . . to that . . . kind of design," she managed to say.

Jed was torn. He wanted to hear Kelly's impressions of the house, yet he wanted to lose himself in the sweetness of her body. He loved having her in his home, knowing she was close. It was an answered prayer for him to be able to drop in on her when it was time for them both to take a break from work, to pull her into his arms and feel her lips under his, to thrill to the eagerness of her response. He let his hands rove at their leisure and decided he could ask her about the house while still thoroughly enjoying the moment. "Did you see the place?" he asked aloud. "Did Tony take you there?"

Kelly arched her body to thrust her breasts against his palms, wishing the thin cotton of her tank top weren't a barrier. "Mmm," she answered vaguely. "It's a wonderful house in a perfect setting. Just like—" She stopped. This was no time to remind Jed of the dreams they'd once had. He'd probably forgotten by now. In any case, when they'd talked about their future, they hadn't thought about Kernaghan dying, about the old white mansion becoming Jed's. She'd loved the house Tony had shown her; it had reawakened old longings. She'd found herself resenting the rich New Yorker who had left all the details of his new home to Tony and probably wouldn't even use the place year-round. It would become one of the grand summer homes around northern Michigan, left all boarded up for most for the year, wasted.

"Just like what?" Jed prompted, tugging Kelly's tank top loose from her shorts. As his hands slid under the shirt to caress her skin, he felt the sudden tensing of her body, a sign of her quickly burgeoning desire. "Just like what?" he asked again, wondering if she would admit that the house Tony had shown her was like the one they'd imagined so long ago.

"Like something out of a magazine," Kelly replied. Her body was catching fire. Jed could always set her aflame with a touch, a kiss, even a look or a word. She wasn't interested in a discussion of houses. She caught Jed's lower lip between her teeth and nipped at it, then stroked it with her tongue.

Jed decided to drop the subject of houses before he aroused her suspicions. Besides, he'd aroused her in other ways, and she'd done the same to him. With a quick motion he slipped her tank top over her head and tossed it aside, then gripped her upper arms and stood back to admire her as if she were a glorious work of art. "You should work this way all the time," he murmured. "Wearing nothing but cutoffs. Very cool, practical . . ."

"I might smear myself with paint," Kelly said playfully.

"I'd be happy to wash it off, sweetheart." Dipping his head, Jed swirled his tongue around each pink crest of her breasts, then stood back again, feeling rather like an artist adding just the right amount of color and texture to a living sculpture. "You know, love," he mused aloud, "there's so much pleasure we've yet to experience together." His voice grew thick with desire. "We haven't, for instance, made love in a shower yet. Or here . . ." He glanced at the couch across the room. "I believe the time is"—smiling, he touched her full, soft breasts—"ripe."

Kelly closed her eyes and leaned into his hands as they gently kneaded her swollen mounds. "Isn't Dorothy still downstairs? It's only five o'clock."

"She left early," Jed answered, moving his hands over Kelly's back and down to cup her denim-clad buttocks. "A cold supper is in the fridge for us, and all the doors are locked. Diane left a while ago too. So here we are, completely alone. You're in my power now, Kelly. How do you feel about that?"

Kelly considered the matter, then slowly, smiling wickedly, moved back, undid her cutoffs and pushed them off, taking her bikinis with them and kicking off her sandals at the same time. "Does this answer your question?" she asked sweetly.

Jed coughed, then cleared his throat before he could speak. "Eloquently," he said at last. "But I believe I had the situation backwards."

Kelly took a step toward him and reached out to pull his polo shirt loose from his waistband. "Backwards?" she repeated. "What do you mean?"

"It should be fairly obvious, Kelly-love. I'm the one who's in your power, not the other way around. As I said once . . . you learn too quickly."

As Kelly slipped her hands under his shirt she closed

her eyes and concentrated fully on the hard expanse of his chest under her palms. "There's a third force at work here," she said gently, smiling as she pulled his shirt off over his head. "One that has us both in its power. It seems to be, as they say, bigger than both of us." She opened her eyes and looked up at Jed. She wanted him, desperately, but her feelings went deeper. She felt such tenderness for him, a strange protectiveness, and at the same time had learned to accept and love his ways of protecting her.

She'd been in his home for three weeks now, discovering a contentment she hadn't known was possible. As good as his word, he'd given her his mother's room as her own, but since he hadn't promised where he'd be sleeping, he joined her there every night and they slept in each other's arms, sated from their lovemaking, closer with every passing day.

"Is your offer still open?" she blurted.

"What offer?" Jed asked, grinning. "Snuggling in bed with books on Celtic lore? Taking a shower together? Washing smeared paint off your pretty breasts? Making love on the couch? All of the above?"

Kelly began trembling as the enormity of what she knew she was about to say and do hit her, but she laughed softly. "All of the above," she replied, "and one thing more."

Jed studied her, not daring to hope. "What one thing more, sweetheart?" he asked in a low voice.

Kelly twined her fingers through the springy coils of hair that formed an inverted triangle on his chest and tapered down to a point under his waistband. She pressed her lips to his shoulder, then whispered, "If you're still interested in marriage, Brannan . . ."

He held his breath. Was he hearing what he wanted to hear, or had she really said . . . ? "What was that, love?" He stroked her naked back, molding her body to his, loving the feel of her against him.

Kelly managed a smile. "If you're still interested in marrying me, I'd like to reconsider my earlier and terribly foolish refusals."

Closing his eyes, Jed folded his arms around her and held her as if all the love he felt for her could pour from his body into hers. "I'm still interested," he said hoarsely.

"Then . . . yes." Kelly's voice had grown stronger. She knew she was making Jed happy and was amazed she could inspire such depth of emotion in him, amazed she could feel so much love for him in return. "I love you," she told him. "I want to be your wife."

Jed stroked her hair and her back, grazing his fingers over the sides of her breasts, tracing the curve of her spine to its base, relearning Kelly's body with renewed happiness.

"'About those other offers," she whispered with a sidelong glance at the couch.

"How could I possibly refuse my fiancée anything she asked?" he said with a chuckle, then lifted her in his arms and carried her across the room.

Jed finally moved over her and relieved the ache he'd created within her, filling her with his heat and hardness, then moving with ever deepening, slow strokes. Kelly felt her deepest core unfolding to him like petals to the rays of the sun.

There were no words between them as they loved each other. Their bodies and their eyes said all that was needed, and at the instant of their summit, they gazed at each other with a love that transcended language and time and space.

When they had finally, reluctantly—and temporarily— drawn apart, Jed held Kelly in the cradle of his body. "Whatever happens next," he said quietly, "whatever kind of wedding we have, whatever the celebrations and ceremonies, I'll always think of these moments as our own private vows. I've already married you, Kelly."

"I know." She nestled against him and smiled. "I'll also be surprised if"—she hesitated, then decided she couldn't hold back from Jed, ever again—"if we aren't parents before too long. Especially after tonight."

Jed was glad she'd finally said it aloud. He'd known since the first night. "It's what you've wanted all along, sweetheart, isn't it?"

She nodded, realizing he was right.

"Even when you insisted you wouldn't marry me?"

She nodded again.

"I guess I'm about to sound like a dumb male, but honey, I don't really understand."

"Neither do I," Kelly admitted. "I guess my drive to be with you, to be part of you . . . seems to have out-weighed my anger and my fears. Oh, I admit I was embarrassed about being a virgin, but sort of glad, too, because there was never anyone for me but you. It was strange how my mind made certain decisions, while my body made totally different ones."

Jed chuckled and hugged her closer. "I knew there was some reason I particularly loved your body."

"I'm still scared," Kelly told him. "I won't let it stand in our way, but if I let myself think, really think . . . something inside me turns to ice. It's a vague feeling of dread I can't shake. I keep telling myself it's some dumb superstition like the foolishness about the banshees."

"I think it goes deeper," Jed said carefully. He'd been giving a lot of thought to Kelly's fears, hoping to help her overcome them. He hadn't expected such open-ness, and he hadn't expected to hear her say she'd marry him—not yet—though he'd felt her resistance melting away by the hour. "You've lost three people you loved deeply, sweetheart. Your parents and Kernaghan.

And it all happened within a couple of years, while you were relatively young. Their deaths have come as shocks to you and created some fears. I've seen how you react when your brother phones, or doesn't phone when you expect him to. You're always braced for some catastrophe, always waiting for the ax to fall. It'll take time to get over that. Maybe loving me has seemed like too much of a risk."

"It does, Jed. It really does. I don't think I could bear it if I lost you."

"But there are no guarantees, Kelly. I'll never leave you, you must know that. The trouble is, I can't promise not to get hit by lightning. But I'll tell you this, if I did, you'd survive. You'd find a way to be happy. You're tougher than you think. It's part of what I love about you."

Kelly thought about his words, then raised her head to frown at him. "Okay. But do me a favor, will you? Don't get hit by lightning?"

Jed laughed. "I'll do my best to avoid it. But I could starve to death. What do you say to dinner?"

"A cold supper suddenly sounds wonderful," Kelly agreed. "Since we're alone, do you think we could skip the formalities of dressing for dinner and just slip into robes?"

"Great idea. There'll be less to take off next time I attack you. Correction: next time you attack me."

The supper was simple and perfect. Cold chicken, potato salad, and crusty bread washed down with white wine was Kelly's idea of heaven. "Hey," she said as she bit into a plump cherry tomato. "I guess this is a celebration."

"Of our engagement?" Jed asked, then frowned. "I don't have a ring. Why wouldn't I have a ring? I've waited long enough."

Kelly grinned. "Aha! I'll bet I know. You've got a few superstitions of your own."

"You're right," Jed said. "Every time I thought of getting a ring for you, I shied away from it because it seemed like I was pushing my luck. Tomorrow I'll get a ring. Do you want to help pick it out, or do you prefer it to be a surprise?"

"I prefer a surprise. It's not the ring I care about, but the fact that you'll have chosen it. By the way, when I mentioned that we were celebrating I was also thinking about the fact that I finished the designs for Beauregarde's portrait. Let's drink to Kernaghan." She raised her glass and waited for Jed to join her.

He did, but began to feel guilty, wondering whether he should tell her the truth about his grandfather's so-called last request. Finally he decided there couldn't be lies between them, even silly, minor ones. "There's something you should see," he told her, and went into his study, returning moments later with a letter. "This was the last one Kernaghan wrote to me," Jed explained as he handed it to Kelly. "He never mailed it. I found it in the desk after the funeral. Read it and try not to get too mad, okay?"

Kelly scowled and began scanning the letter.

Jed watched her expression, hoping he hadn't made a mistake.

She looked up at him when she'd finished the letter, her green eyes wide. "Why you . . . he . . ." She closed her mouth and started again. "I should have known. I should have guessed. There was never a last request. The whole business about Beauregarde was just a scheme he cooked up and you carried out, you pair of . . . of . . . Irishmen!"

"Honey, Kernaghan wanted to play Cupid. I saw no reason why his sudden departure should spoil his fun. Besides, we're happy and you've created three fantastic works of art and . . ." Jed was talking so fast it took him a while to realize Kelly's expression was filled with mirth. "Kelly?" he asked.

She burst out laughing. "That was the dumbest, silliest, goofiest romantic idea anybody ever came up with. If I weren't hopelessly in love with you, I think I'd be insulted that you couldn't do better."

"It was original, wasn't it?"

"And corny."

Jed shrugged. "What else would you expect from me?"

She shook her head and chuckled. "A portrait of a mynah bird? And I fell for it?"

"Could it be you wanted to fall for it?" Jed dared to suggest.

Kelly glared at him for a moment, then nodded. "It could definitely be. But I think I'll be mad at you anyway."

"Why?" Jed demanded.

Kelly tore off a piece of chicken with her teeth, chewing slowly and watching Jed. "Because," she said with a wink, "every time I'm annoyed or ready to fight you about something, you grab me and haul me off to the nearest bed. I plan to get mad at you a lot, Brannan."

He tipped back his head and laughed—and carried her off to bed.

By midnight they'd talked over wedding plans and decided on a small engagement party to be held within a week. They'd chatted about the future and the past and what they would do with Kelly's cottage. "I think we should keep it," Jed stated. "Our kids would have a great time there."

"Or we could sell it. I've had a couple of offers already," Kelly told him proudly. "Good offers."

He raised himself on one elbow. "You've never mentioned that."

"It never came up in conversation. Why?"

He lay back, staring at the ceiling. "When were these offers made, Kelly?"

"The first offer was made a few months ago. Then in early May, as I recall, some man phoned me and didn't want to take no for an answer. He insisted I'd be happier in a condo with all the amenities like a pool and security and—" She stopped, wondering why she'd never made the connection before. "You think he could be behind the anonymous calls?"

"I'm sure of it."

"How so?"

Jed turned and wrapped his arm around her. "I've been doing a bit of detective work."

"I know, and you found out that my cottage wasn't electronically bugged."

"Which made me wonder how your comings and goings were so accurately monitored."

"I've wondered about that myself," Kelly put in, almost enjoying the cloak-and-dagger mystery of it all, now that she was tucked safely away where her tormentor couldn't get at her. "I've been thinking about the fact that the cottage next door has been sitting empty since it was . . ." She blinked and stared at Jed. "Since it was sold in April. Dear heaven, it's a land grab."

He smiled. "Very good, young lady. Go to the head of the class. I checked into the sale. The buyer was actually a company. Then I looked into the property transactions all along the beach. Guess what?"

"People have been selling to the same company?"

"Not quite. They've been selling to different companies, but I have someone investigating those now."

"To find out what, Brannan?"

He chuckled and pulled her a little closer. "Brannan again? I guess it fits the spirit of the conversation. Tough-guy detective stuff, right?"

"You do love to make fun of me, don't you."

He grinned and nodded cheerfully. "But to answer your question—on second thought, maybe I won't answer it. If you want to play Watson to my Holmes, you tell me what we'll find out about those companies."

Kelly didn't ponder the question long. "The names of the people behind the sales."

"Excellent!" Jed cried with exaggerated enthusiasm.

"Elementary, my dear Holmes," Kelly retorted. "Were the sales forced?"

"Encouraged vehemently," Jed replied. "For instance, one former owner I talked to kept running into inexplicable problems like gas leaks and power cuts and busted water pipes. The repairs got to be too much, so he sold. Then there was the fellow who was sick of being burglarized and vandalized. The idea of a security-guarded condo suddenly seemed very appealing. And there was—"

"You've been a busy little fellow, haven't you?" Kelly interrupted. "Without telling me a bit of it, even though I'm at least marginally involved."

Jed lifted a strand of her hair and began toying with it, nibbling at her ear as he responded to her sharp comment. "You've been so happy and relaxed, sweetheart. I didn't know whether I was on the right track, and I'd planned to ask you tonight about offers on the cottage but—" He paused for some serious attention to her earlobe. "But you distracted me," he said a moment later.

A troubling thought occurred to Kelly, worrisome enough to snap her out of her sensual reverie. "When you do find out who's behind those purchases, and possibly behind the calls to me, what then, Jed?"

He stopped what he was doing, lifted his head, and looked off into space. "I'm not sure," he said at last.

Kelly saw the sudden flash of anger in his gray eyes,

and she shuddered. "Nothing violent, I hope," she ventured in a small voice.

The phone rang before he could reply, and when he hung up and turned to look at her, Jed Brannan was so enraged she wasn't sure she knew him.

"What's wrong?" she cried softly.

He stared at her, hardly able to say the words. "You'll want to get dressed in your jeans. Wear a sweater and jacket too. It's cool out. I don't want you to come with me, but I know there'll be no stopping you. You'll stick to me like glue, understand?"

"What is it?" An icy dread settled around her heart. "Michael? Please don't let it be . . ."

"Not Michael. Your cottage. That was Terry MacKay on the phone, Kelly. Your cottage . . ." He cursed quietly. "It's on fire."

Eleven

Kelly watched in mute shock as firemen hosed down the gutted shell that had been her home. Nothing in the cottage had been saved. All her hours of work restoring flea-market furniture had been literally reduced to ashes. The books she'd collected over the years, the little treasures saved from her childhood, the dishes that had been her mother's—all were completely destroyed.

The worst loss was the set of photo albums that held the single tangible remnant of her parents. Every picture she owned or even knew existed had been in those albums. Her brother had none: She'd been the keeper of the memories. Now they were gone.

Kelly was numb. She tried to be glad that she'd moved her business files and designs to Jed's place weeks ago. She tried to be grateful that she was safe. But she couldn't stop feeling guilty that she'd been too cowardly to look at the photo albums, and now she'd never have the privilege.

Jed stood beside Kelly, his arm around her shoulders. He felt the stiffness of her body as despair gripped her. Her silence was frightening. She hadn't even shed a tear. Her expression was as impassive as if she were watching a dull television documentary.

The fire chief walked over to them. "I'm sorry," he said quietly, looking as if he meant it. "The fire was too far gone by the time it was reported."

"You did everything possible," Kelly replied in a low monotone. "Thank you."

The man frowned and glanced at Jed. They both knew Kelly's apparent calm was unnatural.

"Let's go home, honey," Jed urged her. "There's nothing to be gained by staying here."

Kelly turned her head and stared at him as if he were a stranger. *Home,* she thought. *Home.* Her home was a pile of smoking rubble.

As Jed looked into her eyes he felt physically ill, seeing her crawl back into a defensive shell. "Come on, sweetheart," he said gently.

She went with him and got into the car, not once glancing back at the cottage, not saying a word.

The silence was unbroken until they were in her bedroom and Jed reached out to help her off with her jacket. "I can manage," she said as she moved away from him.

Jed was stung by her withdrawal, but he knew he had to understand what she was going through. She needed every ounce of compassion he could muster.

She took off her jacket and hung it up, moving like a sleepwalker.

"Can I get you something?" he asked desperately. "A drink? Some brandy, maybe? Brandy would make you feel better, sweetheart. Or a hot chocolate, my specialty."

Kelly smiled absently as she raked her fingers through her hair, pushing back a strand that had fallen forward. Jed was concerned, she knew. During the past weeks she'd gotten reacquainted with him, with how thoughtful he was, how much fun, how affectionate. Love for him welled up inside her until it was almost unbearable. All she could think of was how tenuous life was. What if something happened to Jed? Everyone and everything she'd ever cared about seemed marked for destruction. Even Mike had been in trouble until she'd stepped back and let Kernaghan take over. Then Kernaghan himself was struck down. She felt like a walking curse.

"Kelly?" Jed prompted.

She realized she'd been staring at him. "Oh, a brandy would be nice," she murmured.

Grateful for the chance to do something for her, anything at all, Jed bounded out of the room.

Kelly sat on the edge of the bed and took off her sneakers and socks, then neatly tucked the socks into the sneakers and put them away. She sat on the edge of the bed again, not sure what to do next.

Jed returned with the brandy and saw her looking as confused as a lost child, and his heart went out to her. "Here, sweetheart," he said, handing her one snifter. "Take a good belt. Doctor's orders."

She smiled and accepted the glass, but sat holding it, once again staring at Jed. What if something should happen to him? What if she really did bring bad luck to anyone she loved? It was an irrational superstition, but what if it was true? Suddenly she understood what that icy dread that had haunted her since Jed had come back into her life meant. Something inside her was telling her she mustn't care for him, mustn't get too close.

"What's going on in that mind of yours?" Jed asked, sitting beside her and taking a healthy swig of his own brandy.

Kelly realized he'd spoken to her, and she started as if coming out of a trance. "Oh . . . nothing. I was . . .

thinking about what has to be done now. Insurance, that sort of thing."

Sure you were, Jed thought. "You haven't touched your brandy."

She looked at it for a while, then raised the glass to her lips and took a tiny sip.

"Why don't we get into bed," Jed suggested. "We're both tired, and I think we could both use a cuddle."

Kelly panicked. She jumped to her feet and moved to the window, looking out at the stars winking in the clear sky as if everything in the universe were perfect. *Perhaps it was,* she thought. Perhaps tonight's fire was a warning, a way of telling her she had to stay away from Jed. "I—I really feel as if I need to be alone tonight," she said in a small voice.

Jed's thoughts raced. Should he leave, respect her need for privacy, for solitude? "No!" he said aloud. "You *don't* need to be alone, especially tonight."

Kelly turned to stare at him, shocked by his vehement refusal.

Jed put his glass on the night table and strode over to Kelly, gripping her shoulders. "Cut it out, Kelly."

She blinked. "Cut what out?"

"You tell me. Why are you slipping away from me? Why the withdrawal? Do you suspect me of having something to do with the fire?"

Her jaw dropped. "Of course not! How could you even suggest such a thing?"

At least he'd gotten more than a robotlike response from her, he thought. "Then why do you insist on being by yourself? I understand that you're shocked, that you're grief stricken over what you've lost, but don't pull away from me, Kelly. We have to face things together."

"No we don't," Kelly said, twisting out of his grasp. "I can't marry you, Jed. I can't stay here. I have to—"

"Tell me why. Give me one good reason why," Jed interrupted, beginning to discern the direction of Kelly's thoughts.

"You know why," she answered, prepared to offer half the truth. "I don't want to love you or anyone. I don't want marriage. I don't want children. I don't want to spend my life agonizing about losing you."

"So you'll throw everything away," he said bitterly. "That makes sense, Kelly, a whole lot of sense. Isn't it a little late to decide you haven't the courage to bear children?"

"Maybe I've opened my eyes just in time."

"And maybe not. But the question is academic, because you're not going anywhere."

Kelly slammed her glass down on the night table. "I'll not only go, I'll go right now. This very minute." She started toward the door, gambling that Jed's high-handedness was all talk.

It wasn't. His hand shot out and his fingers curled around her arm. "I'm not bluffing, Kelly. You once said I was capable of holding you by force, and you were right. I'm not going to let you turn tail and run. This is the time to fight back, not cower in a corner licking your wounds and feeling sorry for yourself."

"You don't understand!" Kelly cried. "And if you think I'm going to give in to you like some submissive little—"

"Get ready for bed," Jed said tersely, though inside he was overjoyed that he'd shaken Kelly out of her stupor. He made a mental note: When all else fails, get Kelly's temper up.

Kelly stared at him, wondering why on earth she'd ever thought he was gentle and sweet. "Go to hell, Brannan!" she shouted, whirling to grab her jacket from the closet and find her purse.

He watched, barely suppressing a grin. He really had her stirred up now.

With her jacket half on and her purse slung over one shoulder, she marched toward the door where Jed was standing. She stopped when she reached him and thrust out her chin aggressively, still struggling into her jacket. "Don't you try to stop me, Brannan."

He couldn't hold back his smile. "Are you planning to wander into Park Place Hotel in the middle of the night? Barefoot?"

She looked down and cursed under her breath, then glared at Jed. "What's it to you?" she asked. "I should think you'd approve of the way I look. You'd love to keep me this way all the time. Barefoot and pregnant, that's your idea of how to handle a woman."

"You've just brought up another perfectly good reason why I won't let you leave," he said calmly.

"I am *not* pregnant!"

"You could be."

"Not a chance. My body wouldn't betray me."

"I assume," Jed said, "we're talking about the same body that instinctively responds to me when your dizzy brain tells you something else?"

"Don't you call my brain dizzy!"

"You're right. It's not dizzy, just a bit confused. What you need is sleep. For that matter, I'm tired myself. Bedtime, Kelly. No more arguments." Jed kicked off his shoes and began removing his clothes.

Kelly turned away, not daring to look at him. Her body—her treacherous, willful body—was too susceptible to his overwhelming masculinity. "All right, I'll stay here tonight," she conceded. "But you're not sleeping with me. And that's final."

Jed laughed quietly, tossing his shirt over a chair and beginning to undo his jeans. He stripped off his jeans and briefs and threw them over the chair with the rest of his things. When he looked at her and saw that she hadn't moved, was carefully avoiding glancing at him, he wondered if he was pushing too hard. Perhaps she really did need to be alone. Perhaps he was being high-handed and insensitive.

Then he thought of how she'd looked during the fire and how she looked with the emerald fire back in her eyes. He decided that getting her riled had been the best move; keeping her that way might stop the depression she was threatening to sink into. "Still not ready for bed, love?" He walked over to stand directly behind her, then grasped the bottom of her sweater and quickly lifted it up and over her head. "Let me help you," he said belatedly, repeating the motion with her T-shirt before she could lower her arms to stop him.

She whirled on him, realizing too late that she'd played right into his hands. Suddenly he pulled her hard against him, and she was assailed by the familiar and wonderful sensation of her skin against his, her soft breasts molding themselves to the sculptured planes of his chest.

Jed held one hand at the small of her back while the other reached between their bodies to undo her jeans. He pushed them off her a moment later, her briefs with them.

"Ready for bed now?" he asked when her whole body was pliant under his hands and her mouth was as eager as his.

She took a deep breath and looked at him with heavy-lidded eyes. "Damn you, Brannan," she whispered.

Jed wasn't in bed when she woke up in the morning. When she checked the clock on her night table she wasn't surprised—it was nearly ten o'clock. She'd slept soundly and, for some strange reason, without dreams. Cradled in Jed's arms she'd been warmed deep inside by brandy and lovemaking.

With the brightness of day and a good rest behind her, she realized how silly her superstitious dread had been. She wasn't a walking curse. Lots of people had endured losses far greater than hers, yet they managed to go on living and to find happiness. Jed had been right not to allow her to wallow in self-pity.

She was definitely having second thoughts about marrying him, however. Justified or not, the man had no right to impose his will on her the way he'd done, refusing to leave her alone when she'd asked him to. When their wills clashed, he was so . . . implacable. Her superstitious fears were gone only to be replaced by perfectly reasonable ones.

After she'd showered, she dressed in tailored white linen slacks and a yellow silk shirt, complete with underwear, panty hose, high heels, and makeup. It was like a ceremonial donning of armor. Jed found it all too easy to coax her out of her clothes or simply strip them off her, especially when she wore casual outfits and minimal lingerie. And once he'd done that . . .

She marched downstairs and into his office, ready to do battle.

Diane Grant was at her desk. When she looked up and saw Kelly she smiled brightly. "You're up, Kelly. Do you feel better this morning? What a terrible thing to happen to your cottage! Just horrible. To think someone set that fire deliberately. I'd hate to be in his shoes when Jed catches up with him. I've never seen anyone look so angry. His eyes turned to cold steel when I gave him the message."

"What message?" Kelly asked, unable to absorb Diane's torrent of words all at once. "What do you mean the fire was set deliberately? I know Jed suspects someone did, but is there proof?"

"Terry MacKay—you know him, right? The policeman. He's a nice guy. I went out with him a few times, and we really got along, but nothing clicked, so we decided we'd just be—"

"What about Terry?" Kelly urged. She was fond of Diane, but the girl had a way of going off in all directions while telling the simplest story.

"He phoned this morning. There's already been an investigation, and it's definite that the fire was set deliberately. It was arson, there's no question."

"How can they be so sure?"

"I don't know. Something about oil-soaked rags, fragments, meant to look like spontaneous combustion, as if you'd cleaned paintbrushes and left the rags around. I don't understand it, except that the trick didn't work because you weren't working at the cottage. All your equipment was here, so why would there be old rags lying around? You really should talk to Jed, because he called Terry and got the details. Jed's been phoning people all morning as if he's running an investigation of his own. As I said, I feel sorry for the guy who did this if Jed gets hold of him. Scary, let me tell you. I sure wouldn't want to be on the receiving end of Jed Brannan's rage." Diane rolled her eyes and shook her hand as if flicking water off her fingers. "Why don't you go right on in? He doesn't expect me to announce *you*." The secretary flashed a brilliant smile. "He sure is nuts about you, Kelly. I'm glad, because you make such a great couple. Tony and I were talking about you two yesterday, in fact. We thought it would be nice if the four of us could get together some time, say for a picnic or something."

"Tony?" Kelly repeated, even more dazed than she usually was from listening to Diane.

"Tony Leonard. You know him, right? You're doing some work for him?" The girl's blue eyes widened, and suddenly her cheeks flushed pink.

Kelly frowned, wondering why Diane seemed so flustered. "I know him," she answered. "I didn't realize you two were going out."

"I met him here," Diane said. Her blush heightened. "He and Jed are . . . old friends. He drops by to visit occasionally. They have lunch, that sort of thing."

"I think I'll go talk to Jed now," Kelly murmured, deciding the secretary was simply excited by the mere mention of the good-looking, charming contractor.

Opening the door to Jed's study, Kelly remembered the day, a few weeks ago, when she'd been paralyzed with nerves at the thought of seeing him after so many years.

Her reaction was much the same now, but for different reasons. Diane's description of him was accurate. He was on the phone, talking in a low voice. When he glanced up Kelly felt a chill go right through her. She was seeing the real Jed Brannan for the first time. His whole body seemed coiled for action, ready to strike as soon as he'd found his victim. *Jed could be lethal*, she thought.

She said nothing. She sank into a chair opposite him, fascinated. This was the Jed Brannan who ran a multinational corporation as if it were a corner store, the Jed Brannan Kernaghan had talked about who would wade right into the most dangerous and difficult situations, and with the force of his will make things right again. Right according to his judgment, of course.

He hung up and smiled at her, his whole appearance changing, warming. "How are you this morning, love?"

She stared at him, stunned by the abrupt change in his demeanor, frightened by the glimpse of his alter ego. "I won't marry you, Brannan."

He grinned, got to his feet, walked around the desk, and stood over her.

"You try getting tough with me and you'll wish you hadn't," Kelly warned him, rising from her chair. Her threats didn't carry much weight, though, when the top of her head didn't quite make it up to his chin.

Still grinning, he heaved an exaggerated sigh, picked up the telephone receiver with one hand, and punched out a number while his other hand shot out to cup the back of her head, his fingers twining in her hair. He held the receiver to his ear and casually dipped his head to deliver a hard, deep kiss that left her dizzy. "You'll marry me," he said quietly, then began talking into the receiver, once again discussing business.

Kelly thought of struggling, but knew it was useless, so she sat back down and listened to Jed's conversation.

Kelly didn't hear very much. His end of the talk consisted mostly of brief remarks that meant nothing to her.

"Great work," he said at one point. "Thanks. What I'd like you to do now is to contact the police. Call Terry MacKay. He'll know what to do with the information." As he hung up he smiled at Kelly again. "You look pretty today. Like a fresh daisy. You seem rested too."

Kelly hadn't expected compliments. "You'll do anything to throw me off track," she said. "I came in here to have a serious discussion with you and—" The phone rang.

Jed shrugged and answered it. As he listened to someone on the other end of the line his eyes narrowed. "Okay. I'll take it from here," he said, and hung up. He looked at Kelly, this time without a glimmer of a smile. "How brave do you feel?"

"What do you mean?"

"Do you want to confront the guy who was calling you?"

"You know who he is?"

"I think so. I can make sure by myself, but I think you ought to be there."

"Why?"

"You'll see, Kelly. Are you game?"

She stood up. "Of course I'm game," she said a little

shakily. She didn't know whether she really wanted to face the man whose voice had tormented her for so long, but she wasn't about to shrink from it and prove to Jed she was a coward. "I'm surprised you'll let me go along. You're usually overprotective."

"I'll be protecting you, sweetheart. Have no doubt on that score." He cupped his hand under her elbow and led her from the study. "We're going out for a while," he said to the secretary. "Take messages, will you?"

Dorothy was in the front hallway as they headed for the door. "Kelly hasn't had a bite to eat this morning, Jed. She should eat before you go dragging her off somewhere."

He turned to glare at Kelly. "Dammit, girl, do I have to spoon-feed you? I thought you'd have had breakfast before you came to see me."

"I'm fine. I'm not hungry."

He looked at Dorothy. "Any muffins?"

The housekeeper nodded. "Of course."

"Wait here," Jed said to Kelly, and raced into the kitchen. He was back a moment later with a glass of orange juice and a muffin. "You can eat this in the car on the way. Thanks, Dorothy."

Kelly was in Jed's car drinking juice and biting into the banana muffin before she had time to think about it. "This is why I won't marry you, you know," she said as Jed backed out of the driveway.

"Because I make you eat like normal people eat?"

"Because you're so damned bossy. Because you simply decide what's going to be done and expect me to fall in line without question."

Jed turned onto the street and shifted into forward. "What's wrong with that?" he asked.

Kelly choked on her muffin and had to take several gulps of juice before she could answer. "Why, nothing's wrong with that! I mean, why should I expect to have anything to say about my life? What Jed Brannan says is law. Who am I to argue?"

"Now you're getting the idea, honey," he said cheerfully.

"I'd like to think you're kidding," Kelly muttered, "but I have every reason to suspect you're not."

"You'll just have to stick around to find out, then, right?" He frowned. "Fasten your seat belt."

Kelly automatically clicked it into place, then realized what she'd done. "See what I mean? Lord, you're an absolute tyrant!"

"Which is what a man has to be if he hopes to stay on even ground with you." Jed was enjoying the exchange. As long as Kelly was battling with him, she couldn't get herself all worked up at the prospect of meeting her enemy face-to-face. "You'd walk all over me and then despise me for letting you do it. And just how do I play the tyrant? I tell you to do up your seat belt? Is something wrong with that?"

"Well, no. But—"

"I run around getting you juice and a muffin and tell you to eat instead of waiting until you're dizzy and have a headache? Is something wrong with that?"

"No, I suppose not. But—"

"I refuse to let you wander out into the street in the dead of night after you've had a tremendous shock. Is something wrong with that?"

Kelly glowered at him. He was winning the argument. "All right, so I was a little upset. But I asked you very nicely to let me be alone for a while, and you wouldn't. You forced yourself on me."

Jed drew the car to a stop at a street corner and turned to look at her, his gaze penetrating. "Was anything wrong with that?" he asked softly.

Kelly looked away as vivid memories flooded back, memories of the way she'd wrapped her legs around his hips, urging him into her, the way she'd showered kisses on his face and throat and chest, the way she'd nestled into his body all night, so glad to be there. "No. Nothing was wrong with that," she said in a small voice. "Which is exactly the problem."

He shook his head and started the car moving again. "What are you really afraid of?"

Kelly thought about his question and suddenly realized that her ever present, nagging terror was gone. She wasn't afraid at all. She'd lost her house, her treasures, even the irreplaceable photographs, and she'd survived. She'd moved on to the next set of problems. She'd made love, she'd eaten a muffin, she'd tried to follow one of Diane Grant's monologues, she'd begun carrying on with her life. She wasn't afraid.

She was mad. Mad because Jed knew her better than she knew herself, understood her so well she couldn't hope to fool him about anything, couldn't expect ever to get away with cowardice.

Jed would never have let her hide from looking at her photo albums. He'd have made her face them until they were a natural part of her life, memories she could enjoy.

Jed would always bully her, but he'd bully her into being everything she could be—including healthy. She downed the last of her muffin and juice and reached into her purse for a lipstick and compact.

"War paint?" Jed remarked with a grin.

She smiled with feigned sweetness. "I wouldn't want to disappoint this creep. I mean, wouldn't it be awful if he'd wasted all his obscenities on some frump?" She smoothed on coral lipgloss and put it back in her purse. "All set for battle now." With a sidelong glance at Jed, she began worrying. "What will you do to this character?"

Jed didn't answer for a while.

"You're capable of violence, aren't you?" Kelly added, really starting to wonder if this confrontation was a good idea.

"If it's called for," he said quietly.

"Is it called for in this case?"

"Maybe."

"Shouldn't we let the police handle this?" Kelly suggested.

"No."

She knew there was no point in arguing, so she fell silent.

They pulled up to an old cottage on a stretch of beach at least half a mile from Kelly's place.

"You think he watched me from here?" she remarked, beginning to get butterflies.

Jed didn't bother to answer. He got out of the car and went around to help Kelly out. "You okay?" he asked.

She nodded, feeling anything but okay.

He led her around the cottage to the beach side. They walked up to the screen door; the inside door was open.

Jed pulled the screen door open, took Kelly's hand, and kept her behind him as they walked into the tiny, ramshackle house.

The door slammed shut, and the noise seemed to echo across the bay. The interior of the cottage was dark, the paper blinds on the windows pulled down.

Jed released Kelly's hand at the same moment that she saw a young man on the tattered couch. Scrawny, clad only in jeans that were too big for him and badly torn, stringy haired, pale, and groggy from what appeared to have been a drugged sleep, the man—boy, really—was trying to sit up and figure out what was happening. He looked up at Jed and Kelly, squinting through swollen eyes and raking his long, thin fingers through his hair.

Jed walked over to him "This is him, Kelly," he said matter-of-factly. "Look familiar?"

Kelly stared at the boy for a long time, then nodded. "Too familiar," she replied. "He did his damnedest to get my brother hooked on drugs two years ago, and he very nearly succeeded."

Twelve

Jed's expression was unreadable as he looked down at the person who'd spent weeks menacing Kelly. "Henry, isn't it?" he said, his voice strained but controlled.

When the boy's only reply was to make a vain effort to focus bleary eyes on his hostile visitors, Kelly supplied the rest of the name. "Henry Webster. Played guitar in a rock band that Michael joined the summer after we lost our parents. Why did you do this to me, Henry? Are you still mad because I didn't approve?"

Henry stared at her for a moment, then spat on the floor. "Hey, lady, I don't give a sweet—"

"Watch it," Jed interrupted. "Watch what you say and watch what you do. Be very polite, all right?" Though he spoke quietly, almost gently, there was enough steel in his tone to send a shiver through Kelly and make Henry cringe visibly. "Miss Flynn asked you a question, Henry," Jed went on. "Why did you make those calls to her? Why did you hide in that cottage next door to hers so you could watch all her moves and try to terrorize her?"

"What calls?" Henry asked, slurring the words. He

reached into the pocket of his denim jacket and took out a cigarette package. Turning it upside down he shook out the one cigarette that was left in it. "Got a match?"

Kelly and Jed exchanged a look. Henry, at approximately twenty years old, was a burned-out wreck of humanity.

"Okay," Jed said, sitting down on the couch beside the boy. "You don't know about the calls. Let's talk about the fire."

Henry had to focus all over again, now that Jed had moved. "Fire?"

"You don't know about that either?"

"I got no idea what you're talking about, mister. And I still got no match." Henry started to get up, patting his pockets in search of a matchbook.

Jed's hand clamped down on his skinny shoulder and brought Henry back to his original position. "Let me fill you in, Henry. Kelly Flynn's cottage was burned last night. You don't know about that?"

"I already said so."

"And you don't know about any phone calls."

"What the hell you talking about, man?"

Jed shook his head. "Leaving dirty messages on an answering machine was cute, Henry. But stupid." He reached into his pocket and took out a tiny tape recorder. "I've just taped you, kid."

Henry scowled. "So what? I didn't say nothin.' "

Jed smiled. "You said enough. Ever hear of voice prints, Henry?"

The boy stared at Jed, then made a lunge for the machine, but Jed simply held it out of his reach and sat back so Henry pitched forward and landed on the floor at Jed's feet, crushing the lone cigarette.

"Clumsy kid," Jed remarked to Kelly.

She stood frozen, sure Jed was going to erupt any

second and do something terrible to the boy. She wouldn't be able to stop him. He was too strong.

Jed put the tape recorder back in his pocket, then reached down and picked Henry up by the seat of the pants, effortlessly placing him on the couch exactly as he'd been before his fall.

Henry's already pale skin turned ashen. Jed hadn't hurt him, but the little display of power spoke volumes. "I don't know nothing about no fire," he squeaked.

"I believe you," Jed said pleasantly. "But the cops won't. You're a prime suspect, Henry. So why don't you just talk to me? Tell me all about the little game you've been playing. And while you're at it, tell Kelly how you knew about the banshees."

"Listen, they wanted me to get real mean about it, like pretending to be the ghost of her old lady or old man."

"You mean her parents, right? Let's have some respect, Henry. It's important that you're very, very polite to Miss Flynn."

"Right," Henry said hastily. "Her parents. Anyway, they told me that'd really scare her, but I didn't do it. I ain't that rotten. I remembered how Mike used to bug his sister about being superstitious. When she'd start in on him about hangin' around with me, he'd just laugh and make these weird screaming noises and say they were banshees. She'd get real upset, man. More mad than scared, but it sure got to her."

"So you heard the storm and thought the wind sounded like Mike's banshees," Jed prompted. "Thought you'd give the lady a good scare."

"They were puttin' pressure on me, see. She wouldn't budge. She wouldn't scare, and I was in trouble for it."

Jed looked up at Kelly. "Honey, why don't you dust off a chair and sit down? I think Henry's got a lot to tell us." He turned to Henry again and spoke gently. "You did it for drugs, right?"

When it was all over and Henry was in police custody, Jed and Kelly drove home in silence.

Kelly was reeling from the day's events. She could hardly absorb the fact that she'd been caught up in a scene triggered by a greedy Detroit land developer. He'd seen her and her neighbors as mere stumbling blocks in the path of his grand plan for a huge tourist complex along the beachfront. He didn't do his own dirty work, though. He used people like Henry. Henry, desperate for drugs and acquainted with Kelly Flynn through her brother, had been easy to persuade into harassing her. Another call, another "fix."

Jed's threatened violence had never materialized, though he'd been menacing enough to get a full confession from Henry, a statement that would have his Detroit employer behind bars for some time to come. Jed, surprising Kelly, had told the police that Henry had cooperated and ought to be put into a drug program. He'd even offered to try to help the boy in any way he could.

Jed Brannan was a complex, unpredictable man, Kelly was beginning to realize. Throughout the summer he'd seemed so carefree and lighthearted, yet he'd hired a private detective and worked doggedly with him to chase down the reasons for the anonymous phone calls. Without telling her, he'd taken the tape from her answering machine, and today he'd had the foresight to have his own small tape recorder with him so he could get Henry's voice. He was unbelievably thorough and determined.

What still stunned Kelly above all was that a pathetic wreck like Henry had terrorized her for so long.

Once again Jed had been right, asking her to confront her tormentor. It had put things in perspective.

She couldn't help thinking that she'd played right into her enemy's hands by being strictly defensive. She should have told Jed at the outset about the calls instead of clinging to her so-called independence. She'd been the perfect victim.

Henry hadn't set the fire, hadn't known about it. His helplessness once she'd moved in with Jed had triggered Henry's boss in Detroit into more drastic action. The man he'd hired was already in custody and talking freely to the police about his employer's activities.

All thanks to Jed. Jed was a man to act, not react.

They pulled into the driveway at his house, and he helped Kelly out of the car. "Tired?" he said, his voice and eyes filled with loving concern.

"A little," she admitted, realizing it was evening.

"Dorothy's left dinner for us again," he told her.

Kelly scowled. "When did you find time to talk to her?"

"When I went to get us the sandwiches and coffee."

Kelly shook her head. "You're scary."

They went up the steps and Jed unlocked the front door. "Why scary?"

"You're so . . . on top of situations, so in control of everything, from uncovering criminals to arranging for dinner. You run your company from Traverse City, for heaven's sake, with about as much hassle as a beach bum gathering shells. You're the toughest man I've ever seen, and you scared the living daylights out of Henry, yet you were practically gentle with him. I was sure you'd tear him apart, but you ended up trying to get him help." She smiled wanly and went into the house as Jed held the door. "The only person I can think of who's remotely like you is . . . was . . . Kernaghan."

Jed put his arm around her shoulders and gave her a quick hug. "You couldn't have said anything nicer to me, Kelly. I spent seven years learning to fill his shoes—or trying to. He taught me to face problems head-on the instant they came up. He sent me into situations where I had to learn to be tough physically and emotionally, but he preached against using violence except if it absolutely couldn't be avoided." He led Kelly to the kitchen and flipped on the light. "Kernaghan never asked his men to do anything he couldn't do himself, and he insisted I had to be the same way. It worked. I've hired loyal people who respect my judgment, so I can trust them to run things without a lot of interference. Life at the top becomes pretty easy for the most part. It's the same in your business, Kelly."

She smiled. "Hardly a comparable situation."

"It's perfectly comparable. You operate on a smaller scale, but the principles are exactly the same. Your employees know you can do what you ask of them. They can't get away with less, because you'll spot any shoddy workmanship. You respect them enough to demand a lot of them. Your only problem is that you started from nothing, with precious little financing to back you, so you have to do too much of the day-to-day stuff that someone else should be taking care of. You've reached the stage where you need computers, and at least one secretary, and—"

"Hang on," Kelly said with a laugh. "You're getting way ahead of me."

Jed smiled. "Like you said, sometimes I let my enthusiasm run away with me. Let's see what Dorothy's left for us tonight."

A savory stew, a loaf of crusty bread, and a bottle of Beaujolais hit the spot for Kelly. She was beginning to accept that her troubles were really over, and as she and Jed tidied the kitchen, she felt herself relaxing as she hadn't in months—years.

They went up to bed early. In her room Kelly began undressing, then suddenly realized Jed was standing at the door, watching her. "Is something wrong?" she asked.

He shook his head. "I've been thinking about the things you said, Kelly. I'm not sorry I refused to let you leave last night, and I'm still going to insist you stay here. But I'll respect your wishes and your privacy, sweetheart. I don't have the right to impose myself on you when you're not sure about your feelings." He crooked his finger under her chin, lightly brushed his lips over hers, and winked. "Good night, love. Sleep well."

Kelly's mouth was agape for several moments after he'd gone. *Now* what was he up to? Had he stopped wanting her?

She finished undressing and crawled into bed feeling terribly lonely and somewhat betrayed. He wasn't supposed to abandon her this way.

Jed lay staring at the ceiling in his room, the room that had been his as a boy. He'd never wanted to use the master bedroom. It was still Kernaghan's, and his mother and stepfather would be taking over the house as soon as they'd had enough of Europe. The master bedroom was theirs.

He wondered what was going through Kelly's mind. He knew he was taking a gamble, but he'd had it with arguing with her about getting married. She loved him; he was sure of that. What she needed was some time alone to think. He only hoped her ache was as acute as his.

The days went by more quickly than the nights for both of them, as Jed worked long hours in his office and Kelly buried herself in her studio doing the designs for the windows Tony Leonard had ordered.

Two whole weeks passed. Jed was friendly, even romantic as he courted Kelly in an old-fashioned way, asking her out for dinner or a movie or just for a walk.

They played tennis, and he let her beat him. They joined Tony and Diane for a beach barbecue. Kelly gradually found herself thoroughly enjoying being part of a couple, a group. She'd been a loner for so long, she'd forgotten how much fun could be had in simple evenings with friends.

But at night Jed would walk her to her bedroom door, gently touch his lips to hers, and leave her.

It became a battle of wills. Would he give in first and come to her bed, or would she invite him? Kelly was sure she would win, sure he still wanted her too much to stay away.

Then it struck her, in the middle of a vain struggle to get to sleep, that if winning meant being apart, she might prefer to lose.

The next day she went shopping. Trousseau shopping. She indulged herself in the sexiest, prettiest lingerie she could find. She tried out several new perfumes and bought three of them. She rehearsed a dozen speeches.

Jed kissed Kelly good night as usual and went to his room feeling a little depressed. His campaign of gentle wooing wasn't getting the results he'd hoped for. He'd been so sure Kelly would realize what they had together.

He lay staring at the ceiling, his whole body tense with suppressed desire and fading hopes. He sat up, deciding to go to her. He could always win her by making love to her. Maybe Kelly was simply the kind of woman who would always have to be pursued.

He was on his feet when he realized it would be a mistake to go to her. The decision had to come from Kelly, from her head and heart as well as her eager body. *Patience, Brannan,* he told himself.

Then he heard the timid, hesitant knock. "Come in," he said, hardly believing it could be happening.

Kelly opened the door and caught her breath. Jed was half reclining on his bed, propped up on one elbow, his chest bare, a sheet pulled up to his waist. He looked like a bronzed god. His eyes were like smoldering coals as he gazed at her, slowly taking in every inch of her body in the sheer pink wispy creation that was her nightgown.

Neither of them spoke or moved or even breathed, each getting lost in the moment, understanding the importance of Kelly's gesture.

Finally Jed broke the silence with a hoarse whisper. "Kelly-love," he said, reaching out a hand to her.

She rushed to him and let him pull her into bed, into his arms. "I'm a dope," she cried, nuzzling into the familiar warmth of his throat. "I don't know why I waited so long."

"You're here now," he murmured, holding her close. "Forgive me for putting us through this, love, but—"

"I know. I understand. It had to come from me, Jed. No more being passive, waiting for events or for you to make decisions for me. From now on I make my own decisions. But after I've been so idiotic, do you still want to marry me?"

"Still, Lord help me," he said with a chuckle that came from deep within him.

Though neither of them would have thought their love could be even more fulfilling than before, it was.

The next morning Jed decided the time had come. He went up to Kelly's studio where she was working on the window designs. "How's it coming?" he asked, giving her a quick, affectionate kiss.

"What do you think of these?" The familiar furrows appeared between her brows as she showed him the rough designs.

"I like what you've done with this High King idea. He looks imposing, interesting."

"And this, for another window?" she asked, pointing to a second sheet of pencil sketches.

Jed smiled. "A fertility goddess. Nice. It softens the effect of the other one but has its own sense of drama. And for a bedroom, it's kind of an intriguing symbol to use."

"I still haven't worked out the third window yet. The Celtic cross seems like a natural, but it isn't all that imaginative or different."

"It's the interpretation that makes the design unique," Jed argued, deciding he'd like a Celtic cross for the last window. "Why don't you work on it and see what you come up with?"

She nodded. "I guess you're right. Sure. Somehow it wouldn't seem right to omit that particular symbol, would it? The cross is such an integral part of the heritage."

"That's the way I feel about it." He took a deep breath and forged ahead. "Why don't we drive out to see Tony? He'd love to have a look at these sketches."

"You think so? You don't think I should wait until I have something a little more polished to show him?"

"He's used to reading blueprints. These sketches aren't nearly as complicated. Let's go, okay?"

Kelly shrugged. "I should change." She looked down at her cutoffs and green tank top. "Get into my business clothes."

"You go ahead while I put these into tubes," Jed told her, starting to roll up the sketches. He was actually feeling shaky. What if she hated the house? She wouldn't, of course, but what if she hated the fact that he hadn't consulted her? "Hurry," he urged, eager to get on with things.

She laughed. "Hurry?"

"You know me, sweetheart. Always impatient."

"I'll hurry," she said softly.

Jed met her in her bedroom just as she was putting the finishing touches to her makeup. "Nice," he said.

She'd gotten used to that particular compliment. It was his understated way of telling her he really liked her outfit. She did too. It was an emerald linen dress which somehow managed to be businesslike and sexy—a whole image change for her. Kelly suddenly felt the confidence to dress as she wished, not as she imagined people expected her to. She grinned. "You look pretty nice yourself, Brannan. But then, you always do in those nubby linen blazers of yours and open-necked shirts. You're a constant temptation to a woman, you know."

"I hope so," Jed answered, feeling oddly shy under Kelly's admiring scrutiny. He knew he was going to have to battle for the rest of his days to keep the balance of power between them from tilting too far her way; he was so much in love with her he was in danger of becoming her abject slave. "All set?" he asked with a slight edge of impatience in his voice. The closer he got to the moment of truth, the more nervous he was.

Kelly gave him directions, wondering how he was going to react to the house. It was so like the one they'd planned.

Her first inkling that she'd been tricked came when she and Jed were too busy talking to remember he needed directions. "How did you know to turn this way?" she asked as they headed up the last twisted road to the point of land where Tony was building the place.

Jed realized his mistake. "Lucky guess," he said lamely.

Her second inkling was stronger: Tony wasn't there, and Jed pulled out a set of keys. He unlocked the door and pushed it open. She stared at him, her eyes huge, and walked inside, her legs suddenly turning to liquid.

Nothing was completely finished, but most of the rooms had taken shape.

As they stepped from the hallway into the huge living room where one whole wall of windows overlooked the bay, Kelly let out a tiny cry and grabbed Jed's hand. "The furniture," she whispered, tears filling her eyes. "The furniture I grew up with."

Jed cleared his throat. "I took the liberty of getting it out of storage, sweetheart. If you don't want it . . ."

She moved through the room, touching the familiar mahogany coffee table, the overstuffed chintz-covered couch, the wing chairs. "Of course I want it," she managed to say, and began rushing through the other rooms. It was all here, all the treasures her mother had loved. The huge dining-room table and hutch, the cane-backed chairs, the bookcases—her parents' furniture, in a home again.

Jed trailed behind her and had to blink rapidly himself as tears streamed down Kelly's cheeks. He held his breath as she walked into the master bedroom.

She stopped in her tracks as a deep sob wracked her body.

Jed put his arm around her shoulders, afraid he'd made a terrible mistake.

"Where . . . ? How . . . ?" She swallowed hard and stared at the photographs perched on the night tables and dressers, the album open on the bed. Her parents. Her mother with Kernaghan. Her father with Michael. Herself with her mother. "I don't understand," she managed to say.

"I felt so terrible that we hadn't taken your albums with us, and even though you hadn't said anything, I knew you were devastated at losing them. It finally hit me that there had to be pictures of your family around

Kernaghan's place. They were all such good friends and all such camera bugs. So I got Diane and Dorothy to go through the house, even the attic, and they found these. They're sort of a wedding gift. I don't want to hurt you, honey, but I thought you might be ready to see them now."

"I'm not hurt," she said as her tears began in earnest. "It's . . . it's wonderful. You're wonderful. Diane . . . Dorothy . . ." She threw herself into his arms and wept as she'd never allowed herself to weep before.

Jed was glad he'd had the foresight to put a box of tissues on the night table. He led Kelly to the bed and sat down with her, handing her one tissue after another as he held her until she was finished crying.

"Thank you," she said when her sobs had subsided. She flipped through the photo album, touched by the effort and love that had gone into putting the collection together. "Thank you so much. For all of this."

"Don't thank me, sweetheart. Thank Diane. Thank Dorothy. Most of all, thank Kernaghan. Which reminds me . . ." Jed reached into his jacket pocket and brought out a small velvet box. "I have to thank Kernaghan for playing Cupid. He left me the best legacy of all—the confidence that you still loved me."

Kelly opened the box and gasped softly. "You remembered the ring. With everything else that was happening, and with all my crazy waffling about marrying you, you remembered the ring. It's so beautiful."

Jed took the gold band with its square-cut emerald surrounded by tiny diamonds and slipped it onto Kelly's finger. "I was particularly pleased with the dress you wore today, for obvious reasons."

Kelly smiled, but her tears began flowing again. "It matches," she said raggedly.

"Your eyes, sweetheart. It matches your beautiful, bewitching eyes."

"I love you so much." Kelly rested her head on Jed's shoulder and heaved a sigh. "And I don't deserve you."

"That's true,'" he teased, enjoying her rare moment of humility while it lasted. "But I'll put up with you—with your stubbornness, your bad temper, your . . ." He couldn't keep it up. "Your sweetness," he said more softly, and bent his head to kiss each of her swollen eyelids. "Your sexiness, your brilliant talent . . ."

Kelly suddenly remembered something. "Those windows," she said, pulling back to look at him, her eyes huge. "Those stained-glass panels. The eccentric New York tycoon is you!"

He nodded. "And I insist on the Celtic cross. I also love the fertility goddess. The High King, I feel, sort of represents the position I'll hold in our household . . ."

"Jed Brannan, you are capable of such secrecy, such duplicity, such deviousness and arrogance, it absolutely floors me."

"Now who's been kissing the Blarney stone, sweetheart? You shouldn't flatter me that way. It'll go to my head."

Kelly looked around the bedroom—their bedroom—again, this time taking in all the details and realizing belatedly that one of her quilts, sold a month ago in a gallery, covered the bed. It was the White Horse design. More modern than ancient, more space-age than relic of a dim and mysterious past, Kelly had worked it in contrasting squares of black and white, repeating the motif so it looked like an abstract design—except to someone who knew what it was. Its drama was enhanced by the massive bed and carved-oak headboard, and Kelly couldn't speak for a moment as she gradually realized how much planning Jed had done, all while he was playing detective, running a corporation, and winning her heart. "You, Brannan," she said slowly, "are really something."

He grinned, relieved that she was happy, and he was beginning to be a little bit proud of himself.

Kelly saw the slight cockiness returning to his crooked smile, and she decided not to fawn over him; he was going to be difficult enough to handle in the years to come. "Really something," she repeated, then suddenly pushed him to the bed, jumped on top of him, and gave him a thorough, punishing kiss. "And I'm going to spend the rest of my life," she added with twinkling eyes, "trying to figure out exactly what!"

Jed's arms curled around her as he decided it was time to inaugurate the bed. He smiled and began undoing the zipper of Kelly's dress. "I guess," he said slowly, "I can live with that."

THE EDITOR'S CORNER

Have you been having fun with our **HOMETOWN HUNK CONTEST**? If not, hurry and join in the excitement by entering a gorgeous local man to be a LOVESWEPT cover hero. The deadline for entries is September 15, 1988, and contest rules are in the back of our books. Now, if you need some inspiration, we have six incredible hunks in our LOVESWEPTs this month . . . and you can dream about the six to come next month . . . to get you in the mood to discover one of your own.

First next month, there's Jake Kramer, "danger in the flesh," the fire fighter hero of new author Terry Lawrence's **WHERE THERE'S SMOKE, THERE'S FIRE**, LOVESWEPT #288. When Jennie Cisco sets eyes on Jake, she knows she's in deep trouble—not so much because of the fire he warns her is racing out of control toward her California retreat, as because of the man himself. He is one tough, yet tender, and decidedly sexy man . . . and Jennie isn't the least bit prepared for his steady and potent assault on her senses and her soul. A musician who can no longer perform, Jenny has secluded herself in the mountains. She fiercely resists Jake's advances . . . until she learns that it may be more terrifying to risk losing him than to risk loving him. A romance that blazes with passion!

Our next hunk-of-the-month, pediatrician Patrick Hunter, will make you laugh along with heroine Megan Murphy as he irresistibly attracts her in **THANKS-GIVING**, LOVESWEPT #289, by Janet Evanovich. In this absolutely delightful romance set in Williamsburg, Virginia, at turkey time, Megan and Dr. Pat suddenly find themselves thrown together as the temporary parents of an abandoned baby. Wildly attracted to each

(continued)

other, both yearn to turn their "playing house" into the real thing, yet circumstances *and* Megan's past conspire to keep them apart . . . until she learns that only the doctor who kissed her breathless can heal her lonely heart. A love story as full of chuckles as it is replete with the thrills of falling in love.

Move over Crocodile Dundee, because we've got an Aussie hero to knock the socks off any woman! Brig McKay is a hell-raiser, to be sure, and one of the most devastatingly handsome men ever to cross the path of Deputy Sheriff Millie Surprise, in LOVESWEPT #290, **CAUGHT BY SURPRISE,** by Deborah Smith. Brig has to do some time in Millie's jail, and after getting to know the petite and feisty officer, he's determined to make it a life sentence! But in the past Millie proved to be too much for the men in her life to take, and she's sure she'll turn out to be an embarrassment to Brig. You'll delight in the rollicking, exciting, merry chase as Brig sets out to capture his lady for all time. A delight!

You met that good-looking devil Jared Loring this month, and next Joan Elliott Pickart gives you his own beguiling love story in **MAN OF THE NIGHT,** LOVESWEPT #291. Tabor O'Casey needed Jared's help to rescue her brother, who'd vanished on a mysterious mission, and so she'd called on this complicated and enigmatic man who'd befriended her father. Jared discovers he can refuse her nothing. Though falling as hard and fast for Tabor as she is falling for him, Jared suspects her feelings. And, even in the midst of desperate danger, Tabor must pit herself against the shadowed soul of this man and dare to prove him wrong about her love. A breathlessly beautiful romance!

Here is inspirational hunk #5: Stone Hamilton, one glorious green-eyed, broad-shouldered man and the hero of **TIME OUT,** LOVESWEPT #292, by Patt

(continued)

Bucheister. Never have two people been so mismatched as Stone and beautiful Whitney Grant. He's an efficiency expert; she doesn't even own a watch. He's supremely well-organized, call him Mr. Order; she's delightfully scattered, call her Miss Creativity. Each knows that something *has* to give as they are drawn inexorably into a love affair as hot as it is undeniable. Just how these two charming opposites come to resolve their conflicts will make for marvelous reading next month.

Would you believe charismatic, brawny, handsome, *and* rich? Well, that's just what hero Sam Garrett is! You'll relish his all-out efforts to capture the beautiful and winsome Max Strahan, in **WATER WITCH**, LOVE-SWEPT #293, by Jan Hudson. Hired to find water on a rocky Texas ranch, geologist Max doesn't want anyone to know her methods have nothing to do with science—and everything to do with the mystical talent of using a dowsing stick. Sam's totally pragmatic—except when it comes to loving Max, whose pride and independence are at war with her reckless desire for the man she fears will laugh at her "gift." Then magic, hot and sweet, takes over and sets this glorious romance to simmering! A must-read love story.

Enjoy all the hunks this month and every month!

Carolyn Nichols

Carolyn Nichols
   Editor
LOVESWEPT
Bantam Books
666 Fifth Avenue
New York, NY 10103